A novel based on the major motion picture

Adapted by Lucy Ruggles
Based on the Teleplay by John Killoran and the
Story by David Diamond & David Weissman

New York

Printed in the United States of America

First Edition
1 3 5 7 9 10 8 6 4 2

Library of Congress Catalog Card Number: 2007906282

ISBN-13: 978-1-4231-1405-5
ISBN-10: 1-4231-0405-1

Chapter One

The student parking lot at Summerton High School was bustling. Cars filled with excited upperclassmen filed in, and boys and girls piled out. This would be the last day all year students would arrive this early and eager—it was the first day of school.

Slightly more nervous but just as excited, wide-eyed freshmen descended from a row of yellow school buses. Among them were two friends, Derek Bogart and Virgil Fox. With wavy, brown hair, dark brown eyes, and a square chin, Derek was decidedly good-looking. Subtly handsome in his own way, Virgil was otherwise Derek's opposite: a shock of blond hair fell across his eyes and, unlike Derek's more athletic build, Virgil was lanky with a crooked but charming smile.

"How's my hair?" Derek asked, already knowing the answer.

"Good," replied Virgil. "Mine?"

"Solid."

Virgil stuck out his hand, and the two boys went through the familiar—and obviously well-practiced—motions of an elaborate handshake. They finished by bumping their fists and saying, in unison, "Scorch!"

Derek surveyed the throng of students. "First day of high school, Verge. We finally made the big time. Free periods, football games, chicks . . ."

Derek trailed off as his eyes landed on two pretty girls by the bike racks. Virgil noticed Derek's chest puff slightly as the girls glanced in their direction.

The constant prankster, Virgil couldn't resist himself. "Uh, Derek?" he said, laughing. "You have a bat in the cave."

"Huh?" Derek asked, without taking his eyes off the girls.

Virgil touched his own nose. "Boogie fever."

Quickly, Derek lowered his head and wiped his nose, but it was too late. The girls spotted the motion and giggled as they walked past.

"And that was just a test," Virgil chuckled. "Had it been an actual emergency . . ." he said with the serious tone of a radio announcer.

Derek shoved him on the shoulder, causing Virgil to laugh harder.

As Virgil continued to laugh, a girl stepped from the last of the school buses and made her way toward them. A tan nicely highlighted Stephanie Jameson's heart-shaped face, and she seemed relaxed and ready for school. Seeing her, the boys stood up straighter, although Derek kept glaring at his friend.

"Aww," Stephanie cooed as she approached them, "their first high school fight! My boys are growing up so fast."

Virgil played along. "Where *does* the time go?"

"Who cares about the past?" said Derek,

starting for the school's wide, front steps. "All I'm thinking about is my social future."

"Well, I don't want anything to change," said Stephanie as she slung her backpack over her shoulder. "I've got my two best guys right here, right now."

"Hey." Virgil brightened. "We should get T-shirts that say, Stephanie's Best Guys: Numbers One and Two. I get Number One, right?"

Stephanie shot Virgil a contagious smile before saying, "Derek, I can't believe you talked me into trying out for cheerleader."

"You'll do fine," Virgil assured her. "It's *him* I'm worried about." He jabbed a thumb in Derek's direction. "He's in full freak mode about football tryouts. Don't worry, bud." Virgil slapped Derek on the back. "I'm going to show up for moral support."

"You mean to goof around?" Stephanie corrected.

"Exactly," Virgil said with a grin.

"You better not embarrass me." Derek said.

"D-rock, I never *try* to embarrass you," Virgil said as he opened the large double doors and they stepped into the fluorescent lights of the hallway. "It just works out that way."

Chapter Two

Judging from the size of the football players standing on the sidelines of the practice field, Summerton High School was going to have a *very* good season.

Coach Nibley was pleased with the turnout. What he was not so thrilled with was the fact that Derek Bogart had just overthrown *another* pass.

"It's all right, Bogart," Coach Nibley grunted. "Just relax."

Easier said than done, thought Derek. He *had* to make the team. His social future was riding on it.

As promised, Virgil was fulfilling his comic duties on the sidelines, joking with some of the players. Out of the corner of his eye, Derek saw Stephanie and the other cheerleading hopefuls watching Virgil from the adjacent field. He turned in their direction in time to catch Stephanie beaming one of her hundred-watt smiles—right at Virgil.

As she did, Stephanie thought she heard something. "What is that?" she asked a friend, who shrugged.

The sound grew clearer. They looked in the direction of the noise. It was the drone of an engine.

"*Look out! Get out of the way!*" someone in the thing coming toward them yelled.

The cheerleaders stared in shock as a souped-up lawn mower came hurtling toward them. Its rider, a scrawny kid in a helmet and goggles by the name of Charlie Tuttle, was waving his arms and trying to shoo people from the vehicle's path. The girls scattered just in time for it to whiz past them.

On the football field, unaware of the escaped lawn mower making a beeline for him, Derek bungled yet another pass. He shook his head in frustration.

"Okay, that's enough for today," said Coach Nibley, tucking his clipboard under his massive arm.

"No, wait," shouted Derek. "I can do this, Coach!"

"Derek, it's all right," Virgil assured him, stepping off the sidelines. "You can come back tomorrow. It'll be fine."

Virgil laid a hand on Derek's shoulder, but was taken aback when he got an icy glare in return.

Derek's fuming was interrupted by the oncoming sound of Charlie's frantic screams as his lawn mower barreled down the field. Assistant coaches sprang from its path as the mower sideswiped a bench and continued along the fifty-yard line.

"My field!" Coach Nibley bellowed. "He's chewing up my field!"

Players lunged after Charlie, trying—and failing—to tackle him.

Virgil squinted at the figure on the lawn mower. "You know who I think that is? That's the kid in our class who's, like, nine years old. They skipped him a bunch of grades because he's supposed to be a genius."

Charlie—who was, in fact, eleven years old—zipped by them, screaming like a wild monkey. "Sorry, sorry, sorry, sorry, sorry . . ." he shouted in his wake.

A moment later, Charlie managed to get the lawn mower under control. He was steering it off the field when Derek readied another ball.

"Dork's going down," Derek said, gripping the football above his shoulder.

"What are you doing, Derek?" Virgil asked with some alarm. "It's fine. . . . See? He's going away."

It was too late. Derek had already released a perfect Hail Mary. The ball soared through the air—fast and true. Right on target, it popped an unsuspecting Charlie in the head, bouncing off his helmet and knocking the puny boy to the ground. The mower toppled to the other side, its wheels spinning, and the football players, including Coach Nibley, exploded in laughter.

"Now *that's* some accuracy," the coach joked.

Three players approached Charlie. As he wiped tears from his cheeks, they picked him up and began to bounce him around, as if he weighed no more than a football.

"Look, he's crying!" shouted the first player. "Little baby," he mocked.

This was unnecessary, thought Virgil, as he ran to Charlie's aide. "C'mon, guys," he pleaded. "Give him a break."

"Oh, yeah?" the second player asked, turning his attention on Virgil. Not waiting for an answer, he shoved Virgil hard.

Looking around, Virgil spotted Derek in the gathering crowd. "Um, D-rock, little help here?"

Derek said nothing as the menacing football player came at Virgil again.

"Don't be shy. . . . D-rock . . . ?" Virgil said, his concern growing.

But Derek, now at the front of the crowd, did nothing. He stood there, frozen.

The sky was turning the purple color of dusk as the last football players left the field. Raising their hands they high-fived each other and laughed heartily.

The reason for their laughter? Virgil and Charlie were lashed to a statue of a ram—the school mascot.

"Thanks for sticking up for me. I'm sorry about how it turned out," said Charlie, craning his neck to look at Virgil.

Students heading home from tryouts and practices taunted the two boys as they passed by. The nice ones stifled their laughter. But Jocelyn Lee, one of the more popular freshman girls, did not bother to hide her amusement. Trailed by her usual posse of pretty—if slightly brainless—girls, she pointed and laughed.

"Don't be silly," Virgil answered Charlie. "Couldn't have gone better . . ."

Well, he *could* have done without the miniskirt and tube top that he'd been forced into. They were starting to itch.

"I'm Charlie Tuttle," Virgil's fellow captive introduced himself.

"Virgil Fox." He turned to see Charlie's face smeared with heavy makeup. He figured his own looked roughly the same. Virgil stuck out his hand to shake Charlie's, but the rope that bound him to the ram's leg wouldn't let him reach.

Virgil sighed. "I have to ask. What is the story with that lawn-mower thing?"

Charlie's face brightened at the question. "I'm experimenting with quantum-accelerated, high-velocity travel as an alternative to riding the bus."

Virgil furrowed his brow. Was this kid for real?

"I always get a hard time on the bus," Charlie explained, "and I hypothesized that a rocket-propulsion lawn mower would help me avoid embarrassment."

Virgil looked at Charlie beneath the caked-on makeup. "How's that working out for ya?"

Chapter Three

Three Years Later . . .

A beat-up car pulled into the senior parking lot of Summerton High School, belching exhaust behind it. It rattled to a stop in an empty spot, and out stepped seventeen-year-old Virgil Fox, followed by fourteen-year-old Charlie Tuttle.

Charlie hustled to keep up with Virgil's long stride. He had a complex gadget in his hands.

"So my emotion modulator is actually allowing me to understand what Albert Felinestein is trying to communicate with his various meows. Isn't it exciting?"

But Virgil wasn't listening. He was watching Derek Bogart's gleaming new SUV roll into the parking lot and be immediately surrounded by an adoring crowd. Derek, in his varsity football jacket, stepped out to greet his admirers. The scene made Virgil equal parts jealous and nauseous.

Charlie waved a hand in front of Virgil's distracted face. "Don't you think, Virgil?" he repeated.

But Virgil continued to ignore Charlie. Stephanie, more beautiful than ever, had just stepped out of Derek's car and made her way to his side. She caught Virgil's eye in the crowd and smiled. It was a large and genuine smile, which Virgil returned. Derek spotted his old friend, too, but instead of a smile, he gave only an icy nod.

Derek and Stephanie moved off with their fellow Populars, and Virgil let out a sigh.

"Virgil? Aren't you excited?" Charlie continued, oblivious to Virgil's internal drama.

Virgil shook it off and turned to his friend.

"Yes, Charlie, I'm very excited that you talk to your cat," he said, dropping his keys into his jeans pocket.

Charlie's gadget emitted a series of high-pitched beeps. "Hmmm . . . heavy readings of sarcasm," he observed drily as he shuffled along beside his friend.

"What do you want from me, Charlie?" asked Virgil as the pair flowed into the crowd of students walking toward the building. "Your inventions always work. But I can only act so interested every time you figure out how to power your house with tartar sauce."

Charlie snorted. As if. "Cocktail sauce."

"Whatever," Virgil said, exasperated. "You know what would get me excited? If you ever invented something useful. And when I say 'useful,' I mean, something that would make me rich or popular. Or both."

The end of Virgil's sentence was swallowed up by the sound of a motorcycle roaring up onto the grass beside them, nearly taking out Charlie.

"Hey . . ." Charlie started, looking up to find

15

his near-death experience was thanks to a biker clad head to toe in leather. Zeke Thompson was a senior—and a seriously scary one at that.

Virgil slapped his hand over Charlie's mouth. ". . . You have a nice bike," he finished. "Lots of shiny chrome, gear thingies."

Zeke, unimpressed, shot them a stony glare and moved on.

The social hierarchy of Summerton High could be mapped using the table arrangements of its cafeteria. At one end of the room was the Cool Table, surrounded by people like Derek and Stephanie. At the other end of the room sat Virgil and Charlie. They had their sidekicks, too, of course—Chester and Eugene.

Virgil surveyed the packed lunchroom, looking longingly at the Cool Table, then back at his own.

"How did it all come to this?" Virgil was in a contemplative mood. "Senior year, and I'm still dining at the Dork Table. . . . No offense, guys. I do enjoy the stimulating conversation. . . ."

He left the "but" to the imagination.

"None taken," said Chester, using his fingers to shove an unidentifiable glob of food into his mouth.

"Let's see," said Charlie, answering Virgil's question, "maybe your plight has something to do with being stripped, dressed in miniskirts, and tied to the school mascot."

Chester licked his fingers. "And that a picture of it made the cover of the yearbook. Three years in a row."

"And was on all the local news stations. And the Spanish channel." Eugene's headgear gave him a lisp that made those facts sound that much more pathetic.

Virgil nodded, considering this information as he pushed away his tray of rubbery, gray school meat. "Ah, yes," he sighed. "The Incident I will one day be explaining to an expensive therapist."

As the boys sat picking glumly at their food, a girl approached. Jeanette Pachelewski was a junior and cute in an unconventional way. Her style tended toward the wild and, Virgil hoped, ironic.

"Hey, Sugar Flakes," she said, leaning in toward Charlie.

"Guh . . . Wuh . . . Suh . . ." Charlie gurgled unintelligibly in response.

"That's Charliespeak for 'hello,'" Virgil translated for his tongue-tied friend. "Why do you call him Sugar Flakes?"

"Because he reminds me of one of those cute little plastic action dolls you get in a cereal box." Jeanette winked and moved on.

Virgil smiled. Charlie had matured since his days as a scrawny, eleven-year-old freshman—he'd grown into his nose and finally convinced his mother to let him pick his own clothes—but there was still nothing about him, Virgil thought, that brought to mind action figures.

"Jeanette's been sweating you for two years. What's your deal?" Virgil asked.

"Forget it," Charlie insisted, shaking his head. "I'm married to science."

Virgil rolled his eyes. Across the room, he

spotted Stephanie at the soda machine. "Pardon me, gents," he said, leaving his tray for Charlie to clear as he made his way to her.

Stephanie stood, staring at the soda machine, her cup poised.

"The eternal conundrum in life," Virgil said, coming up behind her. "Do I get the new and improved soda with lemon? Or the *really* new and improved soda with lemon and tofu?"

Stephanie laughed. "So how are you, Verge? I didn't see you much this summer."

In truth, he hadn't seen her much the past *three* summers.

Virgil leaned on the edge of the silver soda machine. "Oh, you know, I was doing a lot of mountain biking, Jet Skiing . . ."

"Video games?"

"Didn't leave the couch . . . So how 'bout you?"

Stephanie flicked her hair behind her shoulder, and Virgil thought he caught a faint hint of something flowery. Or was it fruity? Whatever it was, it smelled good.

"The usual," she said, rolling her eyes.

"Cheerleading camp, pool parties . . . but I did take this awesome architecture class." Her eyes brightened.

"That's cool," said Virgil. "I remember when you made that gingerbread house that had, like, ten rooms."

"Ugh. I'll never eat another two-story colonial."

They both laughed as the bell for the next period rang.

"Well," Stephanie said with a sigh, "I have Calculus. . . . Hate it. Need it. Can't be an architect without it."

"Yeah, I got Public Speaking," said Virgil. "Hate it. Need it. Can't be a game show host without it."

Stephanie smiled, and Virgil caught another whiff of her scent—coconut, definitely—as she hurried to catch up with Derek.

Chapter Four

The next day, Virgil slouched down in his chair, trying to pay attention as, at the front of the room, the teacher attempted to enlighten his history pupils about the Enlightenment. Next to him, Zeke was carefully carving the letter *Z* onto the top of his binder with a screwdriver. He looked up to catch Virgil staring at him. Virgil quickly looked away.

"Jocelyn," the teacher's voice interrupted the collective student daze, "is it too much to ask that you *not* do your nails while I lecture?"

In the third row, Jocelyn Lee had already

painted one hand a metallic, frosty pink. She looked up at her teacher with wide eyes. "Sorry. When are you done?"

The teacher shook his head in frustration and prepared to launch into a familiar lecture on respect when a knock at the classroom door interrupted him.

Charlie stood in the open doorway. "A.V. Club emergency," he said, flashing a laminated paper badge. "I need Virgil Fox right away!"

A quiet chuckle passed through the classroom as Virgil stood.

"I'm moving to Paraguay," he whispered to himself as he left the room.

Charlie was already halfway down the hall, pushing an A.V. cart with a slide projector. Virgil didn't hurry to catch up with him.

"Remember that rocket-propulsion lawn mower I had back on the day of the Incident?" Charlie asked over his shoulder.

"Thanks for mentioning the Incident again. It's been almost ten minutes since someone brought it up," Virgil said.

Charlie gave a nod, indicating Virgil should catch up. Virgil jogged a few halfhearted steps until he was beside him.

Charlie lowered his voice slightly. "Listen, it ties together. That invention may not have been a success, but one element of the design was proved viable." Charlie glanced nervously around the hall, making sure he and Virgil were alone. "The quantum accelerator. You remember when I was on that physics/new reality/Many Worlds Theory kick?"

Virgil snorted. "Yeah, that was fun."

Charlie ignored him. "Well, I started building my own theory based on all of that work, incorporating my proven hypothesis of quantum acceleration. Then I put one of the school's computers on permanent reserve. . . ."

Stopping in front of the computer lab, Charlie looked seriously at Virgil. "And moments ago . . ." He paused for effect. ". . . I uploaded the last piece of the puzzle."

Charlie swung open the door to the computer lab, revealing a room full of kids at work on rows of PCs and Macs. Seeing them, Chester stood abruptly and saluted. "Commander Fox on the bridge!" he squeaked.

The rest of the group followed suit.

Reluctantly, Virgil saluted back. "I really wish they wouldn't do that," he whispered to Charlie.

Charlie settled at a computer at the back of the room. "What I'm about to show you," he said to Virgil, speaking slowly for emphasis, "is very, very, very top secret. We have to keep this just between us."

Virgil nodded, and Charlie pushed a button. The monitor blinked and then sprang to life. "Check it out."

There, on the screen, was a three-dimensional graphic representation of a grid structure. As Virgil watched, streams flowed from either side of the screen, disrupting the grid and causing it to twist and bend in the center, eventually producing what looked like a small hole. Numbers flashed across the screen so quickly Virgil could barely read them. Then, suddenly, the hole sealed, the streams disappeared, and the grid regained its original structure.

"What you're looking at," Charlie said, swiveling in his chair to face Virgil, "is a *successful simulation of practical time travel.*" Charlie's cheeks were flush with excitement and his eyes nearly bugged out of his head.

Virgil stared at his friend skeptically. Then he turned and headed out the computer lab door, causing the remaining nerds to stand and salute again.

Charlie chased Virgil out the doors and toward the parking lot, his shorter legs hustling to keep up. "Hey," he called. "Yesterday you said I should build something useful. Well, time travel is useful."

Virgil stopped and turned. "Charlie, you're *fourteen* years old. You're two years away from a driver's license, you still call your underwear 'underpants,' yet I'm supposed to believe you could build a *time machine*?"

"Yes!" Charlie howled. "And based on my specifications, a person could travel up to forty-eight *hours* into the past!"

Virgil turned and continued walking to his car. "That's weak."

Charlie's eyes narrowed. "Pardon me, how's your time-travel formula coming along?"

Virgil ignored the jab and jiggled his keys in the car door. He slid onto the sun-warmed seat. Charlie slid in beside him, sitting shotgun.

As they drove through the school parking lot, an increasingly wound-up Charlie gave Virgil an animated crash course in the basics of quantum physics.

". . . It's all about light, right? Nothing moves faster. Well, my hypothesis suggests that you can time-travel on a beam of light. From any light source—even light from a slide projector."

"A slide projector?" Virgil asked dubiously. "A regular slide projector?"

"Did I say regular? No, I did not."

At that moment, Jeanette unexpectedly appeared in Charlie's passenger-side window. He jumped. Jeanette was riding alongside the car on her electric scooter, a helmet squashed over her hair.

"Hey, Fruity Pops!" she said. "What's shakin'?"

Charlie gave a slight, embarrassed smile. He rolled up his window. Virgil, teasing, rolled it back down.

"You have to excuse Charlie," Virgil explained to Jeanette as he slowed the car. "He's nervous around girls."

"No, I'm not!" Charlie protested, crossing his arms in front of his chest and shooting Virgil a look.

"It's cool," Jeanette shrugged. "I like shy boys." She winked and took off, leaving Virgil's car in the dust.

"Okay, look," Virgil said, pulling out of the school's grounds. "I'll make you a deal, shy boy. I'll help you with your time machine, and I'll help find you a hardware guy." Virgil still wasn't sure what that was exactly, but Charlie had mentioned it in his ramblings, so it must be important. "But first time we try it out, we use it for whatever *I* want to do."

Charlie hesitated. "All right," he finally agreed. "But, Virgil, this hardware person we need to find is tricky."

"Why?"

"Because he not only needs to be gifted mechanically, but also—let's say—to require a certain moral flexibility. You know, live on the fringes of society. You know anyone like that?"

Without warning, Virgil slammed on the brakes, causing Charlie to fly forward in his seat, the seat belt catching him as he whacked his head on the dashboard.

"*Ow!*" he cried, rubbing his head.

In front of the car, a motorcycle—with Zeke on it—had come to an abrupt stop at a red light.

Virgil had a lightbulb moment. "What about Zeke?"

"Him?" Charlie asked, still rubbing his head.

Virgil nodded his head. "Yeah. You know at those monster truck shows there's always that giant metal dinosaur that breathes fire and destroys cars? He and his dad build those." Virgil switched to his booming announcer voice,

"Killer-saurus! Fifteen thouuuusand pounds of jaw-crushing force!"

Charlie put his hand up to signal enough. "I get it."

"Look out, folks, it's *CAR*-NIVOROUS!"

Zeke, unaware that Charlie and Virgil were talking about him only feet away, sped off in a cloud of black dust.

He was *just* the guy they needed.

Chapter Five

Excited that her son was bringing someone *other* than Charlie over, Mrs. Fox had laid out entirely too much snack food on the Ping-Pong table in their family's basement. Now, Virgil and Charlie stood on one end. On the opposite end of the table, Zeke was bent over a large, complicated schematic that Charlie had drawn. Albert Felinestein, Charlie's cat, circled Zeke's legs.

"Your cat is freaking me out," Zeke snarled.

"It's not my cat; it's his," Virgil answered, pointing at Charlie.

"His name is Albert Felinestein," Charlie explained.

"That's the dumbest name for a cat I've ever heard." Zeke cracked his knuckles loudly as he spoke. *Pop. Pop. Pop.*

"Couldn't agree more, Zeke . . . Zekester," said Virgil. Zeke gave him a death stare. "I'll stop talking now."

The sound of high heels clomping down the stairs broke the awkward silence. Everyone, including Albert Felinestein, looked up to see Virgil's younger sister, Amy, descend the basement stairs in a feather boa and her mother's sequined, gold evening gown.

"Amy, no!" Virgil shouted. "This is a private meeting."

"Oh, I'm sorry," Amy said casually. "I just came down to watch TV. But Mom did mention you had a new friend over . . . a boy."

Her eyes landed on Zeke, who was busily picking his teeth with a screwdriver.

"Ew, he's gross!" she squealed. "Geez, Virgil, why can't you bring home cute boys?"

"Amy, leave or I'm calling Mom!" Virgil started for his little sister.

"Chill," she said. "I'm outta here. It's like I walked into an ugly contest."

She stumbled on her high heels back up the stairs.

"She's a charmer," Zeke said. He bent down again over the schematics. "This thing—quantum integration to the physical properties of light projection—looks like it could work, man," he said finally.

Virgil and Charlie exchanged a look of pleasant surprise. They weren't sure what they'd been expecting, but this wasn't it.

"So you'll help us construct it?" Charlie asked.

Zeke shrugged. "Why not? I'm always up for a challenge." He selected a ruffled potato chip and dunked it into a bowl of bean dip. A large chunk dropped onto his chin as he ate it.

"Uh, you have a little . . . some bean . . ." Charlie shyly reached to wipe the glob from the surprised Zeke's chin.

"Do that again," Zeke growled, "and I rip your lips off and use them for bait."

Charlie gulped and nodded. "Deal."

Chapter Six

Two rusted-out trucks rested on cinder blocks at the entrance to Thompson's Scrapyard, surrounded by an impressive array of debris and scrap metal. A pit bull barked wildly as it yanked against its chain.

Zeke, Virgil, and a rather uncomfortable Charlie, who much preferred cats to dogs, were gathered around the parts of a disassembled slide projector. But this was no ordinary slide projector. The body of the machine was connected to a tangle of wires and colored tubes. Four identical aluminum pods were attached to the mainframe with copper wiring.

Zeke stood, wiping his brow. "So, have you

guys thought how we're going to use this thing?"

Virgil also straightened. "The first journey back through time will obviously be a monumental event, and our specific goal on that journey should be appropriately grandiose." He pushed a stray strand of blond hair out of his eyes and looked at Zeke and then Charlie. "Two words, gentlemen: *the lottery*."

"Nice," Zeke nodded in approval.

"No!" Charlie seemed almost disgusted at the idea. "I refuse to agree to that."

"Oh, but you already did," Virgil said. "You said that if I helped you, we'd use the time machine for whatever I wanted to. No backsies."

Not concerned at the moment with the ethics of the situation, Zeke took a step back from the contraption for an appraising look. "Y'know, you're not gonna be able to just plug this thing into a wall outlet. This is gonna take some major ampage."

"Don't worry about it," Virgil said confidently. "I know where we can get our power source."

* * *

Vice Principal Tolkan was a stern, hard-edged man who took his job way too seriously. At the moment, he stood in front of the vending machine by the teachers' lounge, considering whether to go for pretzel nubs or animal crackers.

Virgil, Charlie, and Zeke carefully approached him. Virgil cleared his throat. "Mr. Tolkan, we need to talk to you about starting a new club."

The vice principal kept his eyes on A16 as he tried to insert a dollar into the money reader. "No can do. We're maxed out on classroom space. The Future Fonduers of America was the last one in."

Charlie bent closer to the machine, cupping his hands around his eyes to get a better look. "Uh," he said, alarmed, "is that Chester inside the vending machine?!"

Sure enough, inside the machine, Chester's round face was flattened against the Plexiglas. He was trying to say something, but the smoosh of his cheeks made what might have been "hey, fellas" sound more like "huflas."

Unconcerned by his student's plight, Mr. Tolkan turned and asked, "Does anyone have four quarters? It's not taking my dollar."

Virgil furrowed his brow. "Aren't you going to do something?" he asked, pointing to his friend suspended between two sugary snacks.

Mr. Tolkan glanced back at poor Chester. "Like what? Change how high school works? Everything in the world has an order. There are those who stuff others into vending machines, and those who get stuffed into vending machines. It's just the way the system works. . . . It's in the vice principals' handbook," he snickered.

"Let's blow this cracker box," said Zeke. The vice principal clearly had some issues.

The boys started to leave reluctantly when Virgil turned back to Mr. Tolkan. He fished in his pocket.

"Perhaps this will help you remember some unused space for our club . . ." he said, dropping four quarters into the vice principal's open palm.

Mr. Tolkan smirked. "Perhaps it will," he said.

Then to Chester, "Scooch to the right. I'm going after the pretzel nubs."

Later that afternoon, their footsteps echoed loudly as the three boys felt their way down a dark, underground hallway. The walls were slightly damp, and the occasional spiderweb tickled their faces.

"The north wing of the old building," Charlie explained above the loud squeak of the A.V. cart's wheels, "was knocked down to make space for the football field, which we're underneath now."

Virgil glanced up at the low ceiling and imagined football practice, led by Derek, coming crashing down on their heads. He shifted the heavy bag of equipment he was carrying to his other shoulder and picked up the pace.

At the end of the hall, they came to a rusty, dungeonlike door that lead to the classroom Vice Principal Tolkan had begrudgingly given Virgil for his club. Undaunted by its appearance, Zeke heaved at it with his shoulder, and the door creaked open, revealing a large, dark, slightly scary room. The thick layer of dust that covered the wooden chairs and desks suggested the janitor had not visited in a number of decades.

Virgil stepped inside, plopping his bag on the concrete floor. "I was hoping for a clam-shaped Jacuzzi," he said smartly, "but I'll take it."

Virgil sat on a musty, tan couch in the corner of what was currently being transformed into their new, as-yet-unnamed club's headquarters. As Charlie and Zeke worked, he occasionally peeked over the pages of his magazine and offered "suggestions." A power station there, a computer over here.

Earlier that day Zeke had stood guard, arms crossed over his chest, as Virgil and Charlie plundered the school computer lab for equipment. The poor computer nerds had watched curiously and helplessly as the machines were carted away, power cords trailing.

They'd even managed to steal the coffeepot

from the teachers' lounge, literally from under Vice Principal Tolkan's nose.

Now, back in the basement, Virgil made another suggestion and Zeke gave him an icy glare. Then Zeke pulled the goggles he'd lifted from the science lab over his eyes and set to work fusing the exposed electrical panel of a broken fax machine to the temperature sensor of the coffeepot. Sparks flew as he brought the blowtorch down.

Meanwhile, Charlie was attaching a wireless router to his laptop. They were almost up and running, just a few more adjustments . . .

"Hey, buddy, while you're up, you mind grabbing me a soda?" Virgil asked from the couch, signaling to Charlie.

Charlie sighed but tossed him an orange soda from a cooler they'd brought from the Fox home.

Finally, after many hours and many trips to the computer lab, science lab, janitorial closet, teachers' lounge, and the Fox and Tuttle homes, the boys had a fully operational time-travel headquarters. The room, full of machines and computers, buzzed and whirred as blank monitors awaited instructions. In the middle sat the souped-up slide projector, with four pods attached by a mess of cords and wires. It was Go Time.

Charlie synchronized one of the monitors with the palm-size computer he held in his hand. Zeke and Virgil, a stopwatch around his neck, stood a few feet behind Charlie.

"Okay," Charlie said with nervous excitement. "Hang on to your hats. . . ."

He pushed a button and the projector rattled as it shot forth a beam of light, not against the wall like a normal projector, but vertically, straight up from the center of the carousel. Around the beam swirled a wavering, shimmering vortex, like a tornado of liquid light—a time vortex. The three boys stepped back in awe, their mouths hanging open.

Charlie held out his hand to give Virgil a clumsy version of his and Derek's old handshake. "Scratch!" Charlie called at the end.

"It's 'scorch,'" Virgil corrected. But he was too astonished to pay much attention to his friend's mistake.

"Right."

"So." Virgil blinked. "Who should be the world's first time traveler?" There was a hint of apprehension in his voice.

"I just ate a meatball sandwich," Zeke said, patting his stomach as he continued to look at the intimidating beam of swirling light. "I might get cramps."

Charlie was not eager to jump in either. "I'm wearing the wrong shoes, otherwise . . ." He turned his attention to the computer.

Virgil glanced around, his eyes coming to rest on Albert Felinestein. The cat, peacefully unaware of the vortex before him, was licking his paws. Virgil swooped him up in his arms, grabbed the goggles from Zeke, and fastened them on the cat's small head. Then he pulled the stopwatch from his neck and hung it around Albert's. Tying one end of a bungee cord to the cat's collar and the other to a metal pulley,

41

Virgil tossed the animal into the vortex. Albert Felinestein disappeared.

Charlie turned back from his computer. Immediately, he sensed something wrong. "Where's Albert Felinestein?" he asked slowly. Then snapping to Virgil, "Did you . . . ?"

A faint, echoey meow filtered from the swirling vortex.

"Are you out of your mind?!" Charlie lunged for Virgil. "He could die!"

Virgil pushed him off. "Oh, but it's okay for me to die?"

Charlie started to smack at Virgil with his open hands.

"Hang on!" cried Zeke. He yanked the bungee cord, and the vortex spit out the cat— frozen solid. Albert Felinestein landed with a clink and skittered across the concrete floor.

"A 'cat-sicle'!" Virgil exclaimed in amusement.

"You idiot," Charlie scolded. "Time travel is unpredictable. The temperature can be highly variable!"

The younger boy looked as if he was about to

cry. He and Virgil began to bicker as Zeke leaned down to retrieve the frozen feline.

"Uh . . . guys?" Zeke said, putting a stop to the duo's quarrel.

Charlie and Virgil turned to see Zeke holding Albert Felinestein—alive, well, and very, very wet.

"Take a look at the stopwatch," Zeke said as Charlie claimed the cat from his arms.

Charlie looked down at the timepiece. "Eight forty-three."

Virgil grabbed the handheld computer and read its clock. "Eight forty-four."

"An exact one-minute differential . . . that means . . ."

"Your cat is the first time traveler in history!" Virgil yelled.

"We did it!" Charlie and Virgil shouted, jumping up and down and hugging each other. Finally, noticing Zeke's disquieting stare, they unclasped and collected themselves.

Virgil cleared his throat. "I mean," he said in a deeper voice this time, "we did it."

Inside a laboratory, two scientists sat facing a bank of computer monitors. "That's peculiar . . ." Dr. Connors said, sitting up in his chair. The monitor directly in front of him was beeping with activity. ". . . I just got a reading that was pretty much off the charts in the Summerton area. You think they got anything upstairs about that?" Connors asked, swiveling to face his colleague.

Dr. Winthorpe, a chubby scientist a few years Connors' junior, was currently munching on a bagel.

"No." Dr. Winthorpe shook his head, crumbs falling from his lab coat to the desk in front of him. "They would've called right away. It's probably another computer error. You know they give us basement dwellers the lame-o equipment. . . . Plus, all the good snacks are upstairs," he added, turning back to his bagel with an air of disappointment.

It would be nice if something—anything— would happen.

Chapter Seven

Virgil sat by himself at one of the long, wooden tables in the school library. His half-completed chemistry homework lay in front of him, but he wasn't studying. Instead, he was concentrating on Stephanie—who seemed to be having equally as hard a time getting work done, with Derek and his football crew standing around her table. Trying to be discreet, Virgil listened in on their conversation.

"Right. Jocelyn Lee is tutoring you in French. That's all?" Stephanie asked, looking up at Derek with skeptical green eyes. "*Mon petit ami a un cerveau a fromage,*" she recited in French.

"See," Derek said, putting his hand on Stephanie's shoulder, "that's why I need help. I don't know what you said."

"I said, 'My boyfriend is a lying cheese brain.'"

Derek leaned down close to Stephanie and lowered his voice, so that Virgil had to strain to hear what he said next. "C'mon, Stephanie. Jocelyn's hot, but she's a total bottom-feeder. I'd never go there. Trust me."

He looked at his girlfriend with pleading, puppy dog eyes. Virgil could see Stephanie reconsidering.

"I know," she said finally, giving Derek a weak smile.

"I'll call you later, okay?" Derek bent down again to give Stephanie a quick kiss and then headed out of the library, followed by his pack of teammates.

Virgil saw his chance. Nonchalantly, he stood up and wandered by Stephanie's table.

"Oh, hey, Steph. I didn't see you in here." Virgil thought he feigned surprise rather well. "I was just looking for a pencil sharpener."

Virgil almost hit himself. Why did he need an excuse to talk to an old friend? Three years ago they would have come to the library together. But now . . .

"Oh, I have one," Stephanie said, fishing in her purse and pulling out a small sharpener.

"Um . . ." he patted his pockets, feeling his cheeks begin to redden, "I thought I . . . Do you have a pencil?"

Stephanie grinned. "Same ol' Verge," she sighed, producing a pencil as well. "Never changes."

"Well, you haven't changed either. . . . Does your hair still frizz up after you run through the sprinkler?" Virgil asked, referring to the first memory of Stephanie that popped into his mind.

"Totally." Stephanie replied, playing along. "This morning before school I set it up on the front lawn . . ."

"Oh, I do love the sprinkler," Virgil said fondly. "Remember that time I almost drowned?"

"Because Derek shoved the nozzle up your nose."

Virgil laughed. "And then he tried to run

away and cracked his head on the telephone pole."

Now they were both laughing. "I miss us," Stephanie said, her laughter fading.

"The three amigos," Virgil smiled.

Stephanie was silent for a moment, and then, looking seriously into Virgil's eyes, she said, "You know, Derek really did try to stop those football players."

Virgil sighed. The moment was over.

"Anyway," Stephanie continued, "I know he feels really bad about what happened that day. . . ."

Virgil nodded but still didn't speak.

"You know, they say that people who don't let go of the past die faster . . . and get more acne," she added.

A tiny smile crept to Virgil's face, and the warmth of the one he got from Stephanie in return almost made him forget what they were talking about. Almost.

Chapter Eight

Virgil, Charlie, and Zeke had been hard-pressed to locate their winter clothing. Virgil had spent an hour digging through the boxes in the back of his closet, but had finally found the needed items.

Now the guys stood in their headquarters decked in puffy parkas, wool scarves, and big, bright mittens . . . in the middle of September.

"I'm sweating like five hogs." Zeke's voice was muffled through the thick scarf he'd wound tightly around his neck.

"Due to the varying irregularities in temperature, I thought we should be prepared," explained Charlie. A trickle of sweat made its way down the side of his flushed face.

At the table, Virgil was trying in vain to tear a page out of the newspaper while still wearing his mittens. He fumbled with the thin paper.

"Okay," he finally said, managing to rip the paper and stuff the folded scrap into his jacket pocket, "I got today's winning lottery numbers."

Charlie synchronized his handheld. It let out a series of short beeps.

"In order to guarantee that the vortex maintains stability long enough for us to return safely," he said sternly, "we're only going to have ten minutes on the other side. . . . Otherwise, we run the risk of exploding."

Virgil stifled a laugh. "That's funny, I thought you said 'exploding.'"

"I did. Activating grid . . ."

Charlie pushed some more buttons, and the beeps sped up. Lights on several of the machines started blinking. Zeke reached into his bag and pulled out a grappling hook.

Virgil gave Zeke a befuddled look. "What's with the grappling hook?"

"You making fun of the hook?" Zeke asked.

"No. Love the hook."

Suddenly, the beam of light burst out of the projector. It began to spin, gaining speed.

"Next stop," Virgil said above the noise, "Funky Town."

One after another, the boys leaped into the twisting vortex, hooting with excitement as they went. Their bodily forms bent and twisted, spinning in the vortex. Then they were shot upward, disappearing in a fantastic torrent of light.

Throughout the school, lights flickered above confused teachers and students as, in their empty basement headquarters, Virgil, Charlie, and Zeke were spit out of the vortex, landing on their faces.

"We'll have to work on our landings," said Zeke, wincing as he picked himself up from the floor.

Charlie, brushing himself off, looked to a monitor. Then he grinned. "One twenty-seven . . . YESTERDAY!"

"Welcome to the past, boys," Virgil said.

Chapter Nine

Moments later, the three time travelers arrived in front of the convenience store near school. So intent on the goal—getting a lottery ticket—Charlie didn't see the "robot" until he almost ran smack into him. The street performer, spray-painted gold from head to toe, stumbled back a step and emitted a sharp whistling noise.

"Sorry!" Charlie shouted over his shoulder as he followed Virgil into the store. They raced to the counter.

"One lottery ticket, please," Virgil said breathlessly, sliding a piece of paper with carefully copied numbers across the counter.

The clerk barely looked up from her tabloid.

"You have to be eighteen to buy a lottery ticket."

The boys stared at her, stunned.

"Shoot!" Charlie said, kicking at the pavement as the three boys filed, deflated, out of the store.

But Virgil wasn't completely beaten. He approached the gold street performer who was in the middle of his robot routine. "Hi," Virgil started. "We need to ask you a favor. . . ."

The man did a robotic movement, swinging his arm from the elbow and making weird, electronic noises with his mouth. He pointed at the tip bucket.

Virgil pulled a few wrinkled bills from his pocket and dropped them into the container. "We need you," he continued, speaking slowly, as if the man might speak Robot instead of English, "to buy a lottery ticket for us with these numbers." Virgil handed the man the slip of paper. "What do you say?"

Again, the robot swung his arm and jerked about mechanically before indicating the tip bucket.

Virgil rolled his eyes. "Okay, okay, I get it. . . ." He grudgingly fished one more bill from his jeans and dropped it in.

The robot smiled and blew the gold whistle hanging from his neck.

"Oh, no!" Charlie exclaimed, checking his handheld. "We have two minutes to get back to school!"

"New plan," Virgil said to the robot man. "We'll meet you here tomorrow at twelve. Hang on to the ticket until then, okay?"

The robot man smiled and bleeped, and the boys sprinted back toward school.

In his lab, Dr. Connors watched the computer monitor excitedly. He knew he couldn't be wrong this time. There was definitely unusual activity. Excitedly, he jotted down notes from the data on his monitor.

"Okay," he said, turning to Dr. Winthorpe. "That's the second fluctuation, of the same exact magnitude, at the same exact location."

But Dr. Winthorpe wasn't convinced. "I'm

telling you, it's a technical glitch," he explained. "What else could it be? Sonic booms from military testing? We'd know about that. . . . Let's just get back to work, all right?" Then Dr. Winthorpe held up a tangled, yellow yo-yo. "Can you help me unknot this?"

Having leaped back to the present, Virgil, Charlie, and Zeke flew around the corner to meet their robot. Virgil could almost taste his million dollars. But what the boys found when the convenience store came into sight stopped them all dead in their tracks.

A huge crowd had gathered—camera crews, reporters, and passersby jostled each other to get a better look. At the center of all the commotion stood what looked an awful lot like a solid-gold robot with ten microphones in his face.

Virgil felt queasy.

A reporter stepped away from the pack and turned to face her camera. "An incredible story from Summerton this afternoon," she said into

55

the lens. "The winner of the state lottery, announced last night, has turned out to be none other than . . . Robot Man."

Holding up the lottery ticket, the performer did some celebratory robot moves as the boys stood slack-jawed.

What had they done?

Chapter Ten

After gym class, Virgil and Charlie conferred in the locker room. Ever since seeing the now-rich Robot Man, their minds had been racing.

"So tomorrow we go back and get another lottery ticket. This time—" Virgil paused as he pulled his T-shirt over his head.

"No. It's wrong, Virgil," Charlie interrupted. "It's cheating."

Virgil gave a thoughtful frown. "You're right. It is cheating. . . . Okay, new plan. We go on TV with the machine, do an infomercial, sell like eight thousand of them, and BINGO!, we're rich and humongously popular. . . . And they say you can't buy happiness. *Pfft.*" He slammed his locker shut.

Charlie was suddenly, and uncharacteristically, in Virgil's face. "Listen to me. If anyone finds out about this time machine, it will be the end of me, you, and Zeke. The END!"

Virgil, a little freaked, looked down at his friend. "Okay, can you back up?" he asked. Charlie took half a step back. "I have personal-space issues."

Absorbed in the moral and practical issues surrounding the time machine, the two boys didn't notice Chester, wearing nothing but a white towel, emerge from the showers. He opened his locker. It was empty.

"Uh-oh . . ." Chester muttered.

Just then, the bell rang and Charlie and Virgil made for the gym doors, which swung open into the crowded hallway.

"We just have to think outside the box," Charlie continued. "I know that there's an important use for the machine."

Virgil raised an eyebrow. "What's more

58

important than being rich and popular?" Charlie gave him a look. "Kidding . . . mostly kidding."

Behind them, Chester, still wearing the towel, peeked his wet head out of the locker room. Two punky kids with overpriced sneakers and unwashed hair were waiting for him.

"Hey, Chester. Looking for these?" one of them asked, dangling Chester's boxer shorts in front of his face.

Chester's face turned fire-engine red. He grasped for his underwear. "Gimme those!"

As Chester lunged for his clothes, the door shut behind him, catching his towel. He was suddenly aware of a very chilly draft. The crowded hallway turned to stare, and Virgil and Charlie winced in pain for their now-naked friend. The students erupted in laughter as Chester quickly ripped a sign off the wall to cover himself.

Suddenly, as if out of nowhere, Vice Principal Tolkan appeared. "What do you think you're doing, Chester?" he asked angrily.

A flustered Chester mumbled an answer.

"Uh . . . some kids stole my clothes."

Mr. Tolkan grimaced. "Well, I'd like to help you. But that would mean altering the delicate social system here at the school . . . so—" He patted Chester's shoulder. "—good luck."

As Mr. Tolkan left, the punk kids with Chester's clothes doubled over in hysterics. Virgil and Charlie took in the whole disastrous scene. It was like a car wreck—they wanted to look away but couldn't.

Turning to say something to Charlie, Virgil saw a familiar look creep onto his friend's face. It was the one Charlie got when he came up with a new mathematical proof or an invention. It was a look of inspiration. "Wait a minute, Virgil. . . . I just had a brilliant idea."

"You mean . . ." Virgil thought he might be having the same idea. ". . . use the machine to . . ."

"Exactly," Charlie nodded. He awkwardly attempted the handshake, yelling, "Starch!"

Virgil shook his head. "Again. 'Scorch.' Did you read the instructions I e-mailed you?"

Virgil, Charlie, and Zeke stood atop a hill over-looking Summerton High. Below, students swarmed the campus, going about their every-day business.

"Look around, gentlemen." Virgil swept his arm in an all-encompassing motion over the scene below. "We currently exist in a world where mere minutes can make or break a person, affecting the rest of their lives. Take what happened to me, freshman year." He shuddered at the memory. "Had I known that sticking up for Charlie would've ruined my life, I would have never done it."

"Why don't you tell us how you really feel?" Charlie muttered.

Virgil either didn't hear or ignored him, because he continued. "Think of all the kids at this school, like Chester . . ."

Below, Chester was crossing the quad, his head down as students snickered. From this vantage point, he looked small and unusually lonely.

". . . who live in constant fear of humiliation, just because they happen to be smaller, uglier, less coordinated, whatever. . . . But we can change all that!"

"You're saying we become, like, silent heroes to the uncool?" Zeke asked.

Virgil nodded. "The Minutemen must use their powers for truth and justice," he said with bravado, puffing out his chest.

"And who are the Minutemen?" Charlie asked.

"We. Us." Virgil put his arms around Zeke and Charlie's shoulders. "The all-important minutes in time. Clever, right?"

"Sort of," Charlie conceded.

"Not really," Zeke answered, shrugging off Virgil's arm.

At the newly named Minutemen headquarters, Virgil folded a garment bag into his duffel as Charlie worked the monitors and Zeke adjusted the projector. The three were sweating in their thick parkas and scarves.

"Forget it, guys," Zeke said, defeated. "None of these remote-control hookups are gonna take. We're not going to be able to make adjustments on the machine's settings while we're back in time."

"Well, then," said Virgil, "I guess one of us is going to hang back. . . . Not it!" he shouted. There was no way he was going to stay behind to man the machine and miss out on all the fun.

"Not it," Zeke yelled.

"Not it—dang it." Charlie pouted. "This is unfair. I invented the machine!"

"Redo. Not it!" Virgil shouted again.

"Not it!" Zeke followed, lightning fast.

"Not it! Double-dang it!"

The guys proceeded to argue about who would stay behind, unaware that they had a visitor. Jeanette had entered the room and was gazing around with interest. Noticing the girl, the boys grew silent. "Jeanette, what are you doing here?" Virgil finally asked.

"I was looking for a club to join, and I saw yours on Vice Principal Tolkan's list: the *Back to the Future* Fan Club," she answered.

"Oh, right," Virgil said, nodding and looking nervously back at Charlie and Zeke.

"I love that movie . . . though I didn't see it. But I totally love the idea of time travel. It's so science-fictiony." Jeanette grinned dreamily at Charlie.

"Actually, Jeanette, your timing is interesting," Virgil said, no pun intended.

Charlie shot him a warning look. "No, it isn't," he said firmly. "Virgil, what are you doing?"

"Uh, excuse us," Zeke said, ushering Virgil and Charlie aside. They whispered urgently while Jeanette picked at her nail polish. At one point, Charlie gestured heatedly, then seemed to calm down. Finally, they turned back to Jeanette.

"Jeanette," Virgil said, motioning to a dusty desk, "have a seat. . . ."

A few moments later, the carousel on the slide projector spun as the newest member of the Minutemen looked on. The vortex filled the dark room with an amber light. Jeanette stared, awestruck.

"Time travel?!" She exhaled the words in a gaspy breath. "This is so, so, soooo cool!"

"Okay, you know what to do, right?" Charlie checked.

"Sure thing, Honey Bran," Jeanette assured him. "But first we have to do something about those outfits." Reaching over, she shut off the machine.

"That's better," Jeanette said, satisfied.

Virgil, Charlie, and Zeke stood before her in brand-new, state-of-the-art, white snowsuits.

"Where did you get these?" Charlie asked, looking down at the shiny—and stylish—fabric.

"My dad just bought a ski store," she said, shrugging.

Nodding, as though that weren't unusual, the boys pulled down their masks and goggles. Virgil admired his reflection in one of the monitors, turning this way and that. "I've been looking for something formfitting that would highlight my extreme masculinity," he said.

Zeke snickered. "Bro, you're built like my grandma."

"Well, you look like a giant alien," Virgil retorted.

"Hey, cork it," Zeke growled.

"You cork it."

"Virgil, grow up—" Charlie interjected.

"Cork it, Charlie."

"Don't tell Charlie to cork it," Zeke argued.

The guys continued to argue as they jumped, one by one, into the vortex and vanished.

Jeanette heaved a sigh. "I never thought time travel would involve so much bickering."

Chapter Eleven

The events of the previous day in the gym locker room played out like déjà vu: Chester approached his locker in a towel and opened the door to find—nothing. "Uh-oh . . ."

He headed for the doorway and started to peek out when suddenly he heard . . .

"Hold it right there, friend!"

Chester turned to see three men in white snowsuits. One of them was holding out a garment bag.

"Uh . . . are you going to pick on me?" Chester asked. "If so, you'll have to take a number."

"Don't be afraid," one of the suited men—Zeke—assured Chester.

"We're here to help," said Charlie.

Virgil handed the bewildered Chester the garment bag.

In the hallway, the same punk kids waited, ready to pounce.

"Here he comes!" one of them said excitedly as someone swung through the locker room doors.

To their surprise, out stepped Chester—dressed in a brand-new sweatsuit from a hip designer's premier collection.

"What's going on, fellas?" Chester asked casually. He looked down at his clothes in their hands. "Oh, you can keep those. Got me some new threads."

Chester flipped his collar and strutted down the hallway, to the great admiration of passing students.

The bullies looked at each other, their mouths hanging open. Their confusion grew when three figures dressed in head-to-toe white emerged from the locker room, saluted them, and sprinted away.

"Who were those snowsuit guys?" one asked. The other shrugged, speechless.

Down the hall, Vice Principal Tolkan was showing off his new prized possession: an ornate diorama of Summerton High School.

"Not bad, huh?" Mr. Tolkan said, pumping the impressed janitor for a compliment. "Twenty years of service, the board gives you either a gold watch or this baby." He looked at the model lovingly. "My sweet little castle."

The janitor reached out a spotted, old hand.

"Don't touch it!" Mr. Tolkan snapped, pulling it away. "It's delicate."

In the next instant, there was an audible *CRUNCH* as the Minutemen plowed into Mr. Tolkan and his model. Raising himself up from the crushed model, the vice principal fumed as the three mysterious figures disappeared down the hall.

Back in the present, an exhilarated Virgil, Charlie, and Zeke came shooting out of the vortex and landed on the soft mattress they'd brought from Zeke's. As they caught their breath, the vortex shrank into nothing.

"Did we win?" Jeanette asked eagerly.

The guys shuffled to their feet, pulling off their masks.

"Oh, we won all right," smiled Virgil. "We won big."

It had been one small step for the Minutemen, one giant leap for nerds.

Chapter Twelve

The next day, Virgil, Charlie, and Zeke walked tall, but unnoticed, through the crowd of students pouring down the hallway.

Vice Principal Tolkan's voice could be heard crackling over the speakers: "One more thing. Yesterday, a group of students dressed in snowsuits disrupted a gym class. More importantly, they destroyed my precious diorama. Whoever these students are," he continued, his voice increasingly threatening, "I want to make it clear that once they are identified, they will face severe penalties. That is all."

Amused that the Minutemen could stroll the

halls unbeknownst to anyone, Virgil strutted. "Cool. We're outlaws," he said.

"On the run from Johnny Law," Zeke added with a cowboyish swagger.

"Naughty Neds," said Charlie, attempting a dangerous look. Zeke and Virgil raised their eyebrows. "What?" Charlie shrugged. "That's what my mom calls me when I forget to floss."

Zeke just shook his head.

Space Burger was packed. Not surprisingly, the restaurant got its name from its extra-terrestrial theme. Stars and constellations were painted on the dark walls, and mobiles of the solar system hung from the ceiling. Now, after school, the tables were brimming with students.

In a snug corner booth, Derek studied with Stephanie.

"Perfect," he said, pointing to the second page of her English homework, "but I think that's a dangling participle."

Stephanie giggled. "Oh, I hate it when those dangle."

Over Stephanie's shoulder, Derek could see Eugene standing at the counter nervously taking an order from Jocelyn and her girl-friends. The boy all but stumbled over himself as he mumbled through their order.

"Okay, your order number is eighty-three. That'll be just a minute," Eugene said.

Jocelyn furrowed her brow, apparently distressed at the thought of standing and waiting. "Oh, you know what?" She leaned over the counter and gently touched Eugene's hand, causing him to blush uncontrollably. "We're *totally* tired and need to sit down. You think maybe you could bring the food to our table? Bend the rules a little . . ." She read his name tag. "Eugene von Hoserberg?"

Eugene was enraptured. "Uh . . . You bet . . ."

Jocelyn batted her eyelashes. "Great," she said and sashayed away to a booth with her friends.

Derek tracked Jocelyn across the room, their eyes meeting for a brief, flirtatious look.

"Derek . . ." Stephanie began, looking up from her homework. Luckily for him, she hadn't seen the look that passed between him and Jocelyn. Derek quickly turned his attention back to her question about dependent clauses.

Behind the counter, Eugene hustled, clinking glasses and plates onto trays. Jocelyn watched him, amused. Next to her table, another Space Burger employee mopped the floor. Wheeling away the yellow bucket, he propped up a WET FLOOR sign.

Delightedly, Jocelyn whispered to her friends, "Watch this."

She kicked the sign, and it clattered under another table just as Eugene approached with a full tray.

"Here you go, Joce—"

He slipped on the wet floor and tottered backward, his arms pinwheeling as he sought balance. In one painful moment, Eugene was airborne, and in the next, flat on his back and covered in sodas and curly fries. The restaurant erupted in wild laughter.

"Nice one, dork," Jocelyn snickered.

Another kid leaned over to mock him. "Way to go, Eugene."

Slipping in a milk shake as he tried to raise himself, Eugene slid back down, humiliated.

In the back, where no one noticed him, Zeke sat alone with the latest issue of his favorite auto magazine. He had an idea. . . .

"Eugene von Hoserberg," Jocelyn cooed again.

"Uh . . . You bet . . ." Eugene repeated.

"Great," said Jocelyn before crossing the room and eyeing Derek, who sat doing work with Stephanie.

It was all just as it had been yesterday—or rather today, as the Minutemen—thanks to Zeke—were on duty. They scrambled across the street toward Space Burger, just in time to see Jocelyn kick the WET FLOOR sign below the table.

"Here you go, Joce—"

Eugene started to slip, but this time, Zeke

was right beside him. Charlie braced Eugene from behind as Zeke grabbed the tray and deposited it safely in front of a disappointed Jocelyn.

"All right! The Snowsuit Guys!" someone shouted from a booth.

Charlie, still trying to hold up Eugene, tried to smile. But the other boy was heavier than Charlie had anticipated. Charlie stumbled under Eugene's weight, knocking the handle of the mop as he staggered backward.

The dirty, wet mop flew upward and landed, with a squishy thud, in Jocelyn's lap, splattering her and her friends with smelly, brown water.

A number of kids snickered discreetly as the Minutemen made their way back outside and across the street, their duty done.

Chapter Thirteen

In one of Summerton High's classrooms, the blackboard read, "Ski Club" in chalky, white letters. About a dozen preppy kids sat around discussing the merits of parabolic skis.

"All right," Vice Principal Tolkan said, bursting into the room with two security guards behind him, "the jig is up, Ski Club!" His eyes narrowed in triumph. "Or should I say . . . *Snowsuit Guys!*"

But Vice Principal Tolkan had it wrong. . . .

For the next few days, the Snowsuit Guys were the talk of Summerton High School. Their do-gooding lined the front page of the school paper. One girl claimed they saved her from drooling all over her desk when she fell asleep in class. They saved another student from walking out of the restroom with a toilet-seat protector stuck to his pants.

Being rescued by the Snowsuit Guys was suddenly a claim to fame. And down in their headquarters, Virgil, Charlie, and Zeke gave themselves pats on the back.

Still, despite their heroics, something—or someone—was bothering them. At his family's scrap yard, Zeke got the strangest sensation he was being watched. And Charlie was convinced that a black van followed him one day as he walked Albert Felinestein.

Virgil was quick to chalk it up to paranoia, but then he had his own run-in at the convenience store. In the middle of getting himself a soda, he caught sight of a man in a black suit. When Virgil moved into a different aisle, so did the man. And when Virgil ducked behind a display of chips, the man in black did the same. It was too much.

Virgil put down his drink and bolted out of the store. He sprinted through the parking lot, nearly getting hit by Robot Man and his brand-new Mercedes.

What was going on?

Chapter Fourteen

The next day, Virgil passed two security guards at the entrance to the cafeteria. The guards had been popping up more and more lately. The vice principal had put Summerton High School on Code Orange, thanks to the Snowsuit Guys. Posters with their sketches were plastered everywhere, asking for information that would lead to their apprehension.

Virgil got in line behind Eugene, catching the tail end of the conversation he was having with the kid in front of him. "Yeah," Eugene was bragging, "I party with them all the time."

"Who's this we're talking about, Eugene?" Virgil asked.

"Oh, hey, Virgil. It's nobody you know. I'm talking about the Snowsuit Guys."

Virgil stifled a groan. Who was Eugene to put Virgil in his place?

"Yeah, I heard about them," Virgil pressed. "They're, like, total heroes. And I guess one of them, the medium-height guy, is really funny and devastatingly handsome—" Okay, so maybe he was pushing it, but he had to try. . . .

Eugene gave Virgil an odd look and moved off with his new friend.

"And they're called the Minutemen, not Snowsuit Guys!" Virgil yelled angrily after him.

"Geesh," he said to himself as he crossed the lunchroom to a table where Charlie and Zeke were already eating. "Anyone notice that Eugene has copped an attitude?" Virgil asked as he plopped his tray down.

"You want attitude?" said Zeke. "Check out Chester."

At the table next to them, Chester was wearing the sweatsuit the Minutemen had given him and dripping in gold chains.

81

"Am I a trendsetter?" they heard Chester ask the entourage seated at his table. "You tell me, dawg. I mean, who else are kids supposed to look to to set trends? Those doorknobs?" He thumbed his finger over at Virgil, Charlie, and Zeke.

The only thing that kept Zeke from getting up and throttling Chester was Stephanie, who appeared at the table with an excited look on her face.

"Verge, I almost called you last night, but I wanted to tell you in person," she said.

"What's going on?" Virgil asked.

Stephanie was glowing. "I got accepted to U.C. Belmont!"

"Get out!" Virgil grinned.

"They have the best architecture department. But it's not a done deal yet. I applied for a cheerleading scholarship, and they're sending a scout over this week." She bit her lip nervously.

"That's great, Steph!" Virgil beamed.

At that moment, Virgil noticed Stephanie's shirt. In big, black letters was silk-screened the words, Snowsuit Guys Rule.

"Nice shirt," he said slyly.

"Oh, my gosh," Stephanie gushed, "those guys are completely cool."

"You know, a lot of people claim to know them, but trust me . . . I know them," Virgil said coolly.

"Get out!" Stephanie punched him on the shoulder.

"You get out!" He punched her back lightly.

"You!" She punched him hard this time, and Virgil tried not to cringe. The last thing he needed was Stephanie thinking he was a wimp.

"Oh, shoot," Stephanie said, checking her watch, "I have to meet Derek and tell him about the scholarship. See ya, Verge."

She smiled and bounced off happily as Virgil watched. He turned back to the guys, beaming. But then he noticed Charlie looked upset.

"What's wrong, Charlie?"

Charlie hesitated, then spit it out. "There's something I haven't told you about the time-travel formula. . . . As you remember, there was one last piece of the equation that evaded me for several years, until I finally found what I was looking for with an extensive, round-the-clock Internet downloading procedure."

"He was hacking," Zeke explained to a lost Virgil.

"It gets worse," Charlie said warily. "I stole the time-travel program from NASA."

Virgil's eyes widened. "You robbed NASA?!" he cried, causing people at nearby tables to turn and stare.

Charlie grabbed Virgil's collar, dragging him and Zeke under the table. "It's not as bad as it sounds," he whispered. "The files were from the nineteen sixties. They were defunct. Nobody had touched them for *decades*."

"It doesn't matter." Virgil shook his head in disbelief. "This is bad, Charlie. Real bad. We could go to prison."

"Just so you know," Zeke cut in, "if we do go to prison, and we share the same cell, I snore like a chain saw."

Charlie shot Zeke a look. He wasn't helping. "This won't be a problem if we just don't use the machine for a while and lay low."

Virgil, still in shock, shook his head. Not use the machine? But they were the Minutemen—it was their duty! With Charlie's news ringing in their ears, the guys rose from under the table only to find the entire lunchroom staring at them. Virgil gulped. "I dropped a grape."

Chapter Fifteen

As they climbed out of his car a few days later, Virgil and Charlie noticed a somber crowd gathered around Derek's SUV parked in the student lot. "What's going on?" Virgil asked, craning his neck to see.

In answer to his question, the passenger door swung open to reveal Stephanie in a full-leg cast. As Derek helped her out, her eyes met Virgil's.

"Oh, no," Virgil gasped, remembering that U.C. Belmont's cheerleading scout was coming today. The look on Stephanie's face broke his heart. He had to do something.

* * *

"**N**o way, Virgil," Charlie said. "It's terrible that Stephanie fell off the top of the pyramid, but forget it. I mean, we all said that we were being watched, right? The heat is on." It was late that afternoon and Virgil had called an emergency meeting at Minutemen headquarters.

Virgil looked at Charlie imploringly. "Look, if we don't help Stephanie, she may lose out on her scholarship. We *have* to go back."

"You just want to because you have a big, creepy crush on her," Charlie retorted.

"Creepy crush?" Jeanette asked, coming alive. Her hand shot up. "I vote yes!"

"Look, Charlie, you said it yourself: the files you hacked into were defunct. I'll bet nobody even knows they're missing. We won't get caught. . . . Need I remind you? We're the Minutemen, not the Weeniemen."

Zeke and Charlie exchanged a look. They couldn't back down from Virgil's challenge.

Moments later, the Minutemen stood in uniform, facing the swirling vortex.

"Don't be late for dinner!" Jeanette called as they leaped into the time warp.

A door at the base of the football field's press box creaked open. A moment later, Virgil's blond head appeared.

"We've got to be very discreet," he whispered as he scanned the perimeter.

Suddenly, the roar of an engine filled the small space. Virgil turned to see Zeke and Charlie sitting on the motorized janitor's cart. He climbed on just as Zeke kicked it into high gear and zoomed out across the field toward cheerleading practice.

Meanwhile, Vice Principal Tolkan eased his car out of the faculty parking lot. Hearing the noise of the cart, he turned his head to see where it was coming from. In that instant, a Mercedes coming down the street screeched to a halt, just millimeters from Tolkan's car. It was Robot Man. He jumped out of his car, making wild, angry robotic moves. With his back turned, he didn't even see two old women on a tandem bicycle slam into his car and tumble across the front hood. Everyone began gesticulating furiously.

Tolkan was not the least bit concerned with the accident unfolding around him. "Snowsuit Guys," he hissed, seeing the Minutemen hurtling across the football field on the janitor's cart. He took off running. Today was the day! He was going to catch those hooligans red-handed.

Near the field, unaware of the chaos about to ensue, Eugene approached a group of kids playing Hacky Sack. "Hey, dudes. Mind if I 'hack' in?" he asked.

Behind them, the cheerleaders had paused in their splits and flips to form a human pyramid. Stephanie was catapulted to the top. "Woo-hoo!" she yelled, raising her fingers in a victorious V.

As she did so, Tolkan, followed by a couple of security guards, raced on to the field. "Stop! Hold it right there!" Tolkan yelled at the cart, his suit jacket flapping behind him.

Ignoring the vice principal, Zeke made a beeline for the pyramid as Eugene kicked the

Hacky Sack and accidentally sent it flying high and wide.

"Hurry, Zeke!" Virgil cried.

Stephanie barely saw the Hacky Sack coming before it smacked her in the head. She teetered and fell from the top of the pyramid. As she fell, Virgil leaped from the cart, diving through the air. He caught Stephanie and they landed on the ground with a hard thud, unharmed.

Seeing Tolkan closing in, Zeke and Charlie peeled out, spraying dirt on the security guards who had almost reached them. Zeke led them in wide circles across the field.

Back by the now-broken pyramid, Stephanie lay on top of Virgil, nose to nose. He could smell her perfume.

"Wow, I don't know who you are," she said to his masked face, "but you're amazing!"

"Get out!" Virgil said before thinking.

A glimmer of recognition flickered across Stephanie's face. Where had she heard that before?

Virgil scrambled to his feet. As the cart flew past, he jumped aboard, hanging on to Zeke.

"Yeah! Snowsuit Guys!" the football team yelled.

"We're called the Minutemen!" Virgil screamed into the wind, but no one could hear.

Unfortunately, they weren't in the clear yet. They were headed directly for Tolkan! The vice principal dove out of the way and landed on a table full of water cups. The football players and cheerleaders laughed as he lifted his head, his wet toupee askew.

"Giddyap!" Zeke yelled as the Minutemen drove into the sunset.

Chapter Sixteen

Chester swaggered down the hallway, his entourage of newly emancipated—and rowdy—nerds following close behind. As they approached a small cluster of punk kids, one of Chester's followers reached out and knocked the books out of a kid's hands. Tolkan came around the corner just as the heavy books banged to the floor.

"What is going on here?" he demanded.

"Chester and his friends keep harassing us," one of the punks whimpered.

"Shut up, dirt ball," Chester scowled.

"Everyone, settle down," said Tolkan. He turned to Chester. "Last I remember you were at the bottom of the food chain, mister, and I will not have students *leapfrogging* to a higher social status. You're coming with me."

Tolkan ushered Chester away by the arm as Charlie and Virgil passed by, perplexed.

"That's strange," Charlie mused. Then he noticed an interesting headline from a stack of school newspapers. He picked up the top one and read, "'Robot Man Sues Old Ladies.'"

Turning to Virgil, Charlie furrowed his brow. "This is bad, Virgil. We're changing the outcome of things that we never planned on. Our jumps are causing a chain reaction."

"How so?"

"Chester getting in trouble—that's never happened before. And robots suing old ladies? It's a world gone mad!"

The bell rang and students noisily dispersed. Charlie headed off to his class, a worried look on his face. Virgil was alone in the hallway, until Stephanie rounded the corner. When she saw him, her face brightened.

"Virgil, you have a minute?" she asked.

"Sure." He shoved his hands in his pockets nervously.

Stephanie led him to an out-of-the-way corner. "Well, I guess thanks are in order."

Virgil looked at her hesitantly. "For what?"

"For saving me . . . *Snowsuit Guy*."

"What?" Virgil squeaked, trying to control the panic that was rising in his chest.

"Don't even try it, Verge," she said. "'*Get out?*' Please! You, Charlie, and Zeke Thompson are the Snowsuit Guys."

Virgil returned her stare with a blank expression. Finally, he blinked. "All right, listen—" he began.

"I knew it! That is so cool! I figured it out because I started thinking. . . . Those kids you helped, it was always right before something bad was about to happen, just like with me."

"Stephanie . . . C'mon. How could we know when something bad was about to happen?"

"That's exactly what I asked myself. I thought about it and thought about it. . . . Then I finally figured it out."

"No, you didn't," Virgil said, shaking his head. How could she have? Stephanie was a smart girl, but it would take a pretty big leap to come up with time travel. But, maybe she had. Maybe it was time to come clean.

"Yes, I did," Stephanie insisted. "Admit it, Virgil—you, Charlie, and Zeke are . . ."

There was a tense pause.

". . . psychic!" she said as Virgil blurted out, "Time travelers."

Her eyes widened. "Time travelers?! Get out!" She pushed him, hard this time, in her disbelief.

"No, that's crazy," Virgil tried to backtrack. "We're psychic. Definitely psychic."

Stephanie moved closer. "Virgil, you said 'time travel.' Oh, my gosh! How do you do it?" she asked, rapt. "Huh? Huh? Huh?"

Virgil groaned. He was totally busted.

Chapter Seventeen

It was Friday night, and the football stands were packed with cheering fans. A large number of students were wearing their new Snowsuit Guys Rule! T-shirts, and much to Tolkan's displeasure, an advertising banner glared "Space Burger Salutes the Snowsuit Guys" in the end zone.

"Why are we here, again?" Zeke asked from the back row. He was squeezed uncomfortably between Virgil, Charlie, and Jeanette. "I hate crowds. I'm antisocial, remember?"

"Because some poor kid usually embarrasses himself at one of these things," explained Virgil.

The game announcer's voice boomed from the press box. "Six seconds left in this matchup of crosstown rivals. The Hillview Hornets are clinging to a four-point lead as we're coming up on fourth and goal for the Summerton Rams."

On the sidelines, Coach Nibley grabbed Derek by the neck of his uniform. "It's all in your hands, Derek," he shouted so loud the stands could hear. "Put it in the end zone. And remember, no pressure . . . and when I say 'no pressure,' that means 'don't blow it.'" He released Derek onto the field.

Derek took his place at the line of scrimmage. "Blue, twenty-two! Blue, twenty-two!" he yelled. But as he prepared for the snap, he thought he heard the sound of laughter from the crowd.

"Hike!" Derek yelled, suddenly unsure of himself. He took the snap and turned to throw when he saw Chester—in his underwear—streaking across the field.

"WA-HOO! Down with Tolkan!" Chester screeched, sending the crowd into hysterics.

"For a guy with nudity issues, he's really

come full circle," Virgil observed drily from the stands.

Distracted by the pasty figure of Chester barreling down the field, Derek fumbled his throw. The other team leaped into action. After a massive scrum, the ball finally came to rest under a Hillview player.

The announcer's voice echoed across the field. "Derek Bogart loses the ball! And Hillview's got it!"

The referee blew his whistle, signaling the end of the game.

"The Hornets win! What a heartbreaker for Summerton," the announcer hollered.

He didn't need to tell that to Derek—the unlucky quarterback was already kneeling on the field, devastated.

It might not have been going back in time, but the next day Virgil found himself in just as strange a situation: Stephanie and Derek were sitting in his basement.

"I always knew you were gonna do big things,

Verge, but time travel? That's whacked-out, man," Derek said, shaking his head.

"Charlie came up with the idea, but I'm basically the leader. Head honcho. *El capitan*." Virgil tooted his own horn quite easily.

Amy interrupted, bouncing down the stairs in a cheerleading uniform and waving pom-poms. "One, two, three, four . . . don't just sit there, yell some more!" she shouted as she performed a klunky routine.

"Amy—" Virgil said.

"I'm too sassy for my shirt, too sassy for my shirt . . ." she started in on another cheer.

"Amy!" he yelled, taking her pom-poms. "Upstairs!"

Ignoring him, she smiled sweetly at Virgil's guests. "Stephanie, I didn't even see you. It's so weird that you're here. And, oh, my gosh, *Derek Bogart* . . ."

Virgil pushed his annoying sister up the stairs. She went reluctantly, calling behind her, "You are, like, the best football player EVER . . . except for that blown play last night."

"Sorry." Virgil sighed. "I'm trying to talk my folks into caging her when there's company."

Stephanie nodded and took her chance. "So about the game last night, Verge. . . . It was a really big deal for Derek. He feels like he let everyone at school down."

"I *know* I would've won that game," Derek said, pounding his clenched fist into his hand.

"But then Chester streaked across the field and distracted him," Stephanie continued.

"I don't know what's gotten into all the dorks lately," Derek said, truly peeved. "It's like they don't know their place anymore."

Virgil and Stephanie, both put off by Derek's rude comment, shared a look.

Pushing aside a growing feeling of annoyance, Virgil looked back at Derek. He knew exactly why his ex–best friend was here. "So you want the Minutemen to stop Chester from interfering with the game?"

There was a long, awkward pause.

Derek looked strangely at Virgil. "No, man. We want you guys to do it."

"Who are the Minutemen?" Stephanie asked, confused.

"That's us. We're . . ." Virgil started to explain, then gave up. "Never mind. I don't know. . . . I mean, Charlie's going to be a tough sell," he said, leaning forward and resting his elbows on his knees.

"C'mon, Verge," pleaded Derek. "You know, we never really talked about what went down that day our freshman year. I tried to stop them but . . . it was a raw deal, man." He shook his head. "But it'd be cool if we could go back to the way we were. Always chillin'."

Virgil thought for a moment. It would be cool. He could be popular—part of the in crowd. Finally, he held out his hand. He and Derek did their patented handshake like they'd invented it just yesterday.

". . . Scorch!" they said in unison.

Chapter Eighteen

The Minutemen sat in Charlie's bedroom, which resembled a science lab more than a living space. On every available surface, some sort of computer or technological doodad whirred and blinked.

Charlie was on his bed, stroking Albert Felinestein. He looked at Virgil, across from him. "I can't believe you want to help Derek after what he did to you—did to us!"

"Charlie, it didn't happen the way we think, okay? And it's time to move on," Virgil reasoned.

"No. We're not jumping," Charlie responded firmly. "Besides, I've been running some tests, and it looks like our time traveling might be damaging the space-time continuum. That could have serious consequences to our future," Charlie said gravely. "Maybe even the planet."

"Whatever," Virgil argued. "The fact is, what happened to Derek in that game was actually our fault, in an indirect way."

"He's right, Granola Berry," Jeanette chimed in. "Chester's like a different person after you rescued him in the locker room."

"Excellent point, Jeanette," said a satisfied Virgil.

Charlie stood in frustration, the cat leaping from his lap, and paced the room. "Is it me, or have I totally lost control of this project?"

Zeke nodded. "Lost control, bro."

An hour later, the Minutemen were suited up and ready to go. Virgil had a video camera tucked discreetly into the jacket of his snowsuit.

"Activating grid," Charlie said, not pleased as he pushed the now familiar sequence of buttons.

The vortex blasted to life in front of them. Zeke grabbed his grappling hook off the table.

"Ah, yes," Charlie said rolling his eyes, "we mustn't forget the grappling hook."

"Everybody's gotta make fun of the grappling hook, but you'll be sorry," Zeke warned before jumping into the vortex, followed by Virgil and Charlie.

"*Wheee!*" Jeanette squealed, smiling. "I never get tired of that."

She picked up a newspaper from a nearby desk and marveled as the words in the headline began to scramble and change: "Bogart Fumbles in Hillview Heartbreaker . . . Bogearc Fliperin ni Filnal Saxon . . . Bobgeaut Stimble Hilnet, Secreaker Gard Hno . . . Rams Sting Hornets in Final Seconds, Bogart a Hero," it finally read as the boys came blasting back out of the vortex and onto the mattress crash pad.

"Hey, guys," Jeanette said, holding up the new, triumphant headline. "You seen this?"

In the background of the front page photo,

the Snowsuit Guys were tackling an underwear-clad Chester.

Later that night, Virgil, Stephanie, and an astonished Derek sat watching the Foxes' television. On the screen a video of the original game played, showing Chester streaking the field and Derek fumbling, losing the game.

"So because you took this copy of the tape with you when you jumped back in time . . ." Stephanie said, puzzled.

". . . it still exists," Virgil nodded. "Pretty clever, huh?"

Derek rewound to watch the play again. "This is totally crazy! You're the man, Verge. I gotta tell the guys about this."

Virgil and Stephanie both jolted up in their seats. "NO! You can't do that!"

"This has to stay between us, Derek," Virgil insisted more calmly. "It's too big."

"Yeah, I see what you're saying," Derek said unconvincingly. Then he slapped Virgil on the back. "Well, this is a cause for celebration.

Tomorrow night we're partying at my house, and, Virgil, you're definitely coming."

"Oh, I can't," said Virgil. "I have plans with Charlie. The Weather Network is counting down the top-ten hail storms of all time."

He paused, his cheeks growing red. "I didn't realize how lame that sounded till I just said it out loud." He laughed. "I'll be there."

Chapter Nineteen

Derek's house was rocking. It was ablaze from the inside and jammed with students laughing and dancing to music so loud it rattled picture frames on the wall.

Virgil, carrying two sodas, weaved his way through the crowd to where Stephanie sat on the couch.

"Thanks, Verge. Having fun?" she asked as she opened her soda.

"Oh, yeah. I haven't been to a party since I was ten. And I remember some pony throwing up on me."

"Hey, that wasn't my fault Snowball ate all my birthday cake."

They shared a laugh that faded away to an awkward silence.

"So . . ." Virgil said finally, "I guess you're going to the dance Saturday?"

Stephanie shrugged apathetically. "Yeah."

"You don't sound happy about it." Virgil sipped his drink.

"I like going but . . . Derek and I go to every party, every social gathering. It's really a sickness when you think about it." Stephanie rolled her eyes.

"I don't know, being popular seems like a very satisfying way of life to me," said Virgil.

"I'm not so sure of that. Sometimes, I wonder if I chose the right path. I mean, look at you. You don't care that you're . . ." Stephanie faded off and looked down at her hands.

". . . Captain of the dorks?" Virgil offered.

"I wasn't going to say it like that. But it does seem like you guys are always having more fun."

Virgil looked at her in disbelief. "Get out. From our side, it looks like you guys are having more fun."

"Get out." She grinned.

Derek, noticing Stephanie and Virgil bonding on the couch, came over and took a seat between them. Virgil watched as Derek's eyes drifted through the room, finally landing on Jocelyn, whom he winked at. Quickly, Virgil glanced to Stephanie. Talking with another cheerleader, she saw nothing of Derek's flirtation.

Dragging his attention from Jocelyn, Derek threw his arm around Virgil's shoulder. "It is so cool hanging out with you again, Verge," Derek said. "And thank those other guys for me—the big scary dude and the little twerp."

Virgil suddenly remembered he'd forgotten to cancel with Charlie. He checked his watch. Ten o'clock. Charlie was probably already in bed. Oh, well—he'd call and apologize tomorrow.

What Virgil didn't know was that Charlie *was* in bed, listening angrily to Derek's party next door and wondering why his friend hadn't called.

"Charlie, how many more times do I have to

apologize?" Virgil asked as he paced his room, his phone cradled between his ear and his neck.

"Three hundred and twelve times ought to do it," Charlie said drily.

Virgil sighed. "I mean it, Charlie, never again."

"Fine," Charlie said finally. "I forgive you. Look, I'm just really concerned about the time machine and the possible aftereffects—"

Virgil cut him off. "Hang on, Charlie. I've got another call. I'll get rid of them." He clicked over. "Hello?"

Stephanie's voice came sobbing through the phone. "Virgil? I . . . I can't believe . . . I just . . . He . . ." She couldn't get it out.

"Steph, what is it?" Virgil asked, alarmed.

She sobbed, mumbling incoherently.

"All right," Virgil said, switching into hero mode. "I'm coming over. Stay right there." He laid down the phone, grabbed his coat, and headed for Stephanie's.

Meanwhile, on the other line, Charlie was waiting. . . .

* * *

Virgil shakily climbed the white, ivy-laden trellis outside Stephanie's room. He tapped on the window. Stephanie came over, wiping away the tears staining her cheeks. She raised the window, and Virgil climbed in.

"I haven't done this since eighth grade," he puffed, out of breath. He knocked over a CD tower, plastic cases scattering over the carpet. "That wasn't there before." He walked across the room. "So," he said gently, "tell me what happened."

Stephanie's lip quivered as she told him about going to surprise Derek at his house, only to find him kissing Jocelyn Lee in his living room.

"I knew it," Stephanie blubbered between sobs. "I just didn't want to believe it. . . . I feel so stupid." She dabbed a tissue at her eyes.

"Look . . . um . . . I know how much you like pistachio nuts, but in the rush to get here, instead I grabbed a bag of pasta shells." Virgil held the bag of pasta out to her.

Stephanie cracked a smile through her tears. "Do you have any marinara sauce?"

111

Virgil almost started for the window again, to run and get some, before realizing it was a joke.

"It's so nice of you to come over," she said. "I mean it, Verge. You're such an amazing friend."

"Yeah . . . friend," Virgil repeated. The word stung like a paper cut—that someone had just poured lemon juice over.

The phone rang. Stephanie answered it, her nose sounding stuffy. "Hello?"

She listened for a second, then put her hand over the receiver and whispered to Virgil, "It's Derek. He wants to talk it out."

Virgil's heart skipped a beat.

"I'm going to take it," she said, giving Virgil a helpless look. Then, stronger, "I have to end it with him once and for all."

"Okay. Well, good luck." He tried to sound "friend"-ly.

Stephanie smiled at him, and Virgil climbed back out the window.

Meanwhile, Charlie sat on his bed, the phone now warm against his ear. The clock showed he'd been on hold for over half an hour.

"Don't look at me like that," Charlie huffed at Albert Felinestein. "I have pride. . . . I'm giving him five more minutes and that's it."

The cat licked his paw and jumped from the bed.

Chapter Twenty

A woman walking her dog on the Summerton High campus watched idly as her dog sniffed at some grass on the football field. Suddenly, the dog's form fluctuated, froze, and then disappeared into thin air. The woman's bloodcurdling scream could be heard for miles, but not at the intelligence lab outside of town, where Doctors Connors and Winthorpe pointed to their monitors as they spoke urgently to their boss.

"These repeated irregularities are all maintaining half-lives after their primary incidence," Dr. Connors said.

"It's totally Weirdsville," Dr. Winthorpe concurred. "And the fluctuations are coming directly from Summerton High School."

"I have a theory," Dr. Connors said rather reluctantly. "Does the department have contacts at the FBI?"

Their boss tensed.

Zeke sat alone, as usual, at his favorite booth in the back of Space Burger. Unless he was with the Minutemen, he generally preferred solitude. But when two cute girls with black hair and dark eyeliner approached to ask if they could join him, how could he say no? They quickly slid in opposite him and stared.

Finally, one spoke. "Did you really escape from prison, or is that just a rumor?"

Zeke would have laughed, but he was too preoccupied by the mysterious man seated at the lunch counter. He was wearing a black suit and dark glasses and looked very out of place in the restaurant. Zeke followed the man's gaze and saw he was staring intently at Virgil and Derek, seated together at another booth.

". . . You don't know what it's like to be

me, man," Derek was saying. "Great athlete, hugely popular. It's like people expect me to play the field, to cheat, almost."

Virgil wasn't buying it, and the half-eaten pizza in front of them was growing cold. "What's your point?"

"But I didn't cheat. Jocelyn made the first move. So it doesn't really count."

Virgil rolled his eyes.

"I want you to go back in time and stop Stephanie from busting me with Jocelyn," Derek said.

"Why should I?" asked Virgil.

"Because it was a big mistake. Huge. And it'll never happen again, I swear."

Virgil didn't like this conversation. "I don't know. . . . I mean, you really hurt her."

Derek pushed the pizza around his plate. "I know. I feel bad. She's everything a guy could want. . . . And her hair always smells nice, like a rain forest."

"Like coconut," Virgil almost corrected Derek, but stopped himself.

"Look, Verge," Derek continued, "I like that

the three of us have been hanging out again. Like the old days . . . What do you say?"

Virgil was silent, considering. "Let me think about it," he finally answered.

After leaving the restaurant, Virgil was still thinking about it. He walked down the sidewalk, pondering the consequences of what Derek was asking him to do. He didn't get the chance to ponder long.

A black van screeched abruptly to a halt next to him. The door slid open and two FBI agents in suits and sunglasses jumped out, grabbing Virgil and dragging him into the back of the van as he yelped for help.

The windows of the van were dark, so Virgil couldn't tell where they were going. He was finally dragged out and taken into what looked like a conference room.

"I'm tellin' you," Virgil said, struggling against the FBI agents' grip, "you grabbed the wrong guy. But I can give you the names of the two—"

Virgil stopped when he spotted Charlie and

Zeke, already seated at a long table and glaring at him. He winked at them and whispered, "I was gonna give them fake names."

"Yeah, right, Mr. Keep Me on Hold All Night," Charlie grumbled.

They were interrupted by the appearance of an agent with a neck as thick as a tree trunk.

"Good afternoon, gentlemen," the agent began in a businesslike tone. "My name is Agent Rehnquist of the Federal Bureau of Investigation." He stood before them, his chest like a barrel. "And I'm going to let you boys in on a secret . . . a national secret. In 1969, shortly after the Apollo Eleven moon landing, the United States government began funding a number of new scientific projects. One of these was time travel."

He studied the boys for a reaction. "Time travel, huh? That's crazy," they muttered.

Rehnquist continued. "The project turned up little results and eventually was shut down, and the files never again touched. . . ." He spun to look at Charlie. "That is, until a very industrious individual, or individuals, broke into the NASA mainframe . . . using a computer which we traced to Summerton High School."

Sweat was starting to bead on the boys' foreheads. The stress was too much. Charlie had seen enough cop shows on TV to know where this was going. He jumped from his seat. "All right! I—"

Zeke elbowed him in the stomach, and Charlie sat back down.

Virgil came to the rescue. "What my friend was about to say was . . . If you're not going to charge us with anything, then you can't keep us here. It's a violation of our civil rights. . . . That's right, look it up. I took a semester of Government. Got a B minus," he said proudly, hoping he was right.

Rehnquist stared Virgil down. Unfortunately, the kid was right.

Agent Rehnquist watched the three boys get escorted from the building. All was not lost. He knew they could get more information by watching them.

The cell phone of an agent standing next to him rang. "It's the lab," the agent said, handing the phone to Rehnquist. "It's urgent."

Chapter Twenty-one

Safely outside, Charlie stopped to catch his breath. "This is bad," he said, leaning over like he might throw up. "Real bad."

"Yeah, way to go, Naughty Ned," Virgil said sarcastically. "Thanks to you, we got the FBI on our backs."

"Me?" Charlie stood and faced Virgil. "I wanted to stop this whole thing weeks ago! But no, you had to use it for your own personal gain."

"Charlie's right," Zeke said. "Going to parties, hanging out with the Populars . . ."

Virgil turned on Zeke. "Hey, if I remember correctly, you benefited, too. We gave you a life.

Before us, you were just this guy everyone was afraid of."

The argument escalated until Virgil stood alone and watched his two friends walk away. Everything was going wrong.

Later, Virgil lay on his bed, staring up at his ceiling and stewing from his fight. His cell phone rang. The caller ID said "Derek."

"What do you say, Verge?" he asked. "Gonna help me out, bud?"

"Yeah. Sure . . . D-rock."

What did he have to lose?

Charlie was dreaming of a roller coaster when he realized someone was jumping on his bed. He propped himself up to find Jeanette bouncing up and down at his feet.

"Good morning, Raisin Crunch," she said cheerily. "You know, I was thinking—"

"The results!" Charlie cried, bounding out of bed and downstairs to the computer he'd worked at all night.

On the screen was a graphic map of Summerton, centering on the high school. A number of spots appeared. Charlie punched some keys, and the spots turned into dots, which turned into circles, growing in size until they finally converged. Charlie turned pale.

"I'm no scientist," Jeanette said, checking out the monitor over his shoulder, "but that doesn't look good."

Charlie began to stammer. "We created a . . . a . . ."

"Spit it out, shug," said Jeanette.

". . . a black hole."

Chapter Twenty-two

In their temporary headquarters, Doctors Connors and Winthorpe were presenting their findings to an assembly of agents and other important-looking people. The suits sat before a giant computer screen that ran the full length of the headquarters wall. The graphic on the screen looked very similar to the one Charlie had pulled up at home.

Just then, as if on cue, Charlie and Jeanette burst through the door of the conference room.

"I lied!" Charlie yelled. "I stole the formula from NASA, and we've been time-traveling all over the place!"

Agent Rehnquist did not act shocked. "Way

ahead of you, Mr. Tuttle. I'd like you to meet Doctors Connors and Winthorpe from the seismology department at Lab Tech. Doctors, this is Charlie Tuttle. . . ."

"What are you, nine years old?" Dr. Connors scoffed.

"He's fourteen," Jeanette said, a hand on her hip.

Charlie gave her a thankful look and went on. "So you already know about the black hole?" Charlie asked.

That got their attention.

"The *what*?" Rehnquist asked, his large jaw dropping almost to the ground.

"The black hole . . . I knew you were underfunded, but *come on*," Charlie replied, exasperated.

"That's preposterous," Dr. Connors cut in. "We ran the worst-case scenario, but we never came up with—"

Charlie studied the formula on the large screen. "I see five—no, six—decimal points that weren't carried over."

Dr. Winthorpe's face turned a shade of green. "Oops," he muttered, taking his seat.

"Each time we used the machine," Charlie explained, "the rift created in the space-time continuum did not disappear." He moved his finger along the ominous-looking dots on the screen. "Instead, the fluctuations blended together to form one giant black hole. But the worst part is . . . the black hole will spread until it swallows up Summerton. Then the Northwest. Then the entire United States. And so on . . ."

Panic hit the room. The previous hush of shock became the din of alarm.

"How much time till zero hour?" Rehnquist asked, his square jaw set like stone.

"According to my estimates," Charlie said gloomily, "less than *four hours* till the end of the world."

"All right, people," Rehnquist barked, "we're going to Code Red! Get Washington on the phone . . . NOW!"

"There may be a way to fix it," Charlie said as the agents snapped to action. "But it's a long shot."

The two scientists exchanged a desperate glance. "Let's hear it, sir."

Charlie took a deep breath. What did he have to lose—except the world?

Chapter Twenty-three

A crowd of kids dressed in fifties attire—saddle shoes and poodle skirts, leather coats and rolled jeans—crossed the football field toward the school gym. Stephanie and Virgil brought up the rear.

"Thank you for coming with me, Verge," Stephanie said shyly.

"Hey, what are friends for?" Virgil said, the word sticking less in his throat now.

The gym was decorated to the nines. Streamers dangled from the ceiling, memorabilia like old records and photos were taped to the walls, and classic rock drifted over the sound system.

Virgil offered to get Stephanie some punch.

As he ladled the red liquid into a plastic cup, Derek approached. "Everything set?" he asked.

"Yeah," Virgil said halfheartedly.

"Cool. We'll go after they announce the winners." Derek slapped him on the back and moved off, past Stephanie, who gave him an icy glare. Clearly, their relationship was not going to heat back up anytime soon.

"Verge, why are you letting Derek bother you?" she asked as she took her punch from him.

"Steph," Virgil asked thoughtfully, "do you believe that a person's life can change in a single moment? For better or worse?"

"Yeah . . . I guess."

"Well, there's a moment in one of our lives that's about to change. And I don't know if it's for the better or the worse."

"Virgil, I'm not following . . ."

On the stage, Vice Principal Tolkan, dressed as Elvis, tapped on the microphone. It emitted an ear-piercing squeal.

"Attention, everyone. . . . It's time to announce this year's king and queen of the dance!" Tolkan did a horrible impression of Elvis, jutting his hip out and cocking his lip. "Thank you. Thank you very much."

Instead of laughs, he got crickets. "Nobody knows Elvis?" he asked incredulously. "Whatever. Stephanie Jameson and Virgil Fox, get up here. You won."

A spotlight hit Virgil and Stephanie and they moved onto the dance floor.

"This is such a surprise!" Stephanie said.

"Not really," Virgil said with a sly smile. "I went back in time and stuffed the ballot box. I mean, who would vote for me?"

Stephanie considered this as they slow-danced. "I would," she said quietly.

As they swayed to the music, Stephanie felt her heart begin to beat faster. "This is weird," she finally said.

"Yeah . . ." Virgil agreed. "Wait, why?"

"A good weird," Stephanie reassured him. "How can you be friends with someone for a long time and then . . ."

". . . it's different?"

"A good different." Stephanie smiled as their lips moved closer and closer. They were about to kiss, when Derek grabbed Virgil by the shoulder.

"Let's go," Derek demanded. "It's time!"

"You know," Virgil said, breaking free from Derek's grip. "I think I've changed my mind." He moved back to Stephanie.

"Too late. It's a done deal." Derek yanked Virgil away again and dragged him out of the gym as Stephanie looked on, frightened.

Noticing the commotion, people moved off the dance floor. "FIGHT!" one of the football players yelled, and kids poured out of the gym to follow Derek and Virgil outside. Tolkan pursued.

As Derek shoved Virgil across the grounds, he glanced back to see the mob of kids catching up with them. "Aw, man," he said, picking up speed and heading for the bleachers.

Back inside the gym, Charlie and Jeanette found Stephanie.

"Stephanie, where's Virgil?" Charlie asked.

He needed to tell him what was going on.

A shadow of anxiety fell across Stephanie's face. "He left with Derek."

"Why? Don't tell me he's going to jump back in time?!" Charlie said, panicked. "He might make things worse!" Charlie ran off to stop them, followed by Stephanie and Jeanette.

Behind the bleachers, Virgil managed to break free and turn to Derek. "I'm not doing this," Virgil said with conviction. "You don't deserve Stephanie."

"I suppose you do?" Derek snapped.

"I'd certainly treat her better," Virgil growled.

"Shut up, Virgil. You think it's going to happen between you and Stephanie? No way, once she finds out what a little dork you are." Derek's lip curled in a sneer.

Virgil felt as though he'd been punched in the gut. He finally saw Derek for who he really was. And he didn't like it.

"You know, all this time I was hoping we could go back to being friends. But why would I want to do that? You're a jerk. Maybe you always were, and I didn't see it. There's no way I'm helping you get Stephanie back."

"Wanna bet, dipwad?"

Derek grabbed Virgil by the shirt collar and forcefully pulled him along. But again, Virgil yanked free.

"Remember when we were little, and you made fun of me because I got beat up by a girl in karate class?" Virgil asked.

"Yeah. That was hilarious."

"Well, see how funny this is!" Virgil did a flying scissor kick, but instead of landing his foot on Derek's chest, as he meant to, he caught only air and landed on his face.

Derek doubled over in laughter. "Once a loser, always a loser," he taunted.

Virgil picked himself up, gasping for air. "You're right," he said, resigned. "Let's go to the time machine."

But as they turned, Virgil stomped as hard as he could on Derek's foot. Derek doubled over in pain. Recovering quickly, he lunged for Virgil as Charlie, out of nowhere, landed on Derek's back.

The two of them spun in a circle, Charlie's arms and legs flailing.

Virgil tried to grab Derek, but just then Charlie flew off. He landed on top of Virgil, knocking him to the ground.

"Virgil, we have a problem!" Charlie said urgently.

"I know. Derek's about to cream both of us."

"Not that. We have less than an hour to save the planet!"

As Charlie spoke, Derek tried to grab them again but found himself wrapped up from behind in the powerful arms of Zeke. "Easy, cowboy," Zeke said.

By that time, the crowd had caught up and gathered around the bleachers. Tolkan came up, out of breath. Derek immediately pointed to Virgil, Charlie, and Zeke. "Mr. Tolkan . . . *these* are the Snowsuit Guys!"

"Well, well, boys," Tolkan said, rubbing his hands together with pleasure. "Looks like the game is up. Take 'em away," he snarled at the security guards, who made a move for the boys.

"Everyone, freeze! FBI!" It was Rehnquist. He held out his badge.

The security guards stopped dead in their tracks just as another agent, the one from the convenience store and Space Burger, burst in. "Stop! CIA!" He held out another shiny badge.

Yet a third man rushed onto the scene. "No one move!" he yelled. "Bureau of Weights and Measures!"

There was a quiet, awkward moment.

"In the future," Virgil whispered to the last agent, "you should probably go *first*."

Without warning, the ground beneath them began to waver. People lost their balance and stumbled, confused and panicky. The vortex suddenly blasted up through the ground and into the sky. Full-blown pandemonium erupted, students running in every direction.

"We need to get these people out of here!" Rehnquist yelled. "*NOW!*"

Chapter Twenty-four

In Minutemen headquarters, agents and scientists of all kinds worked busily over complicated schematics and made adjustments to the time machine. Virgil, Charlie, Zeke, Rehnquist, Dr. Connors, and Dr. Winthorpe discussed the dire situation.

"So *we're* supposed to go *inside* that black hole and close it?" Virgil asked incredulously.

"That's right," said Charlie. "It's the plan I came up with. We'll take the machine with us and reverse the polarity on the opposite side."

"What?!" shouted Tolkan from the outskirts of the conversation. He had demanded—as vice principal—to be part of the conversation. But now he was wondering if that had been such a good idea. "We can't let these students go alone—they could die!"

Rehnquist stared at him, gravely. "We have no choice. They're the only ones familiar with the equipment. . . . If they don't go, then we *all* could die."

That was a good point. "Godspeed," Tolkan said, quickly leaving.

"You know what?" Virgil spoke up, stepping toward Rehnquist. "I'm the one who messed everything up. I'll go alone. They had nothing to do with it."

Charlie stepped up beside him. "What do you mean, 'nothing to do with it'? I *invented* it."

"I helped," Virgil reminded him.

"No, you didn't."

Rehnquist put an end to their bickering. "Enough. You'll both go."

"They'll be needing me, too, sir . . . and my hook." Zeke produced his beloved hook, and Virgil and Charlie rolled their eyes. Apparently, if he went down, Zeke would go down with that grappling hook.

Police barricades surrounded the football field, blocking off hordes of panicked citizens and pushy reporters. In the center of the field, an enormous black hole loomed ominously. Like a giant whirlpool of liquefied matter, it grew larger and larger, absorbing more material every second.

In their full snowsuit regalia, Virgil, Charlie, and Zeke walked side by side toward the field. Photographers and reporters snapped pictures and shouted questions at them: "Mr. Tuttle, can you tell us how this happened? Mr. Thompson, is it true you've been in jail?" A young girl asked Virgil to sign her autograph book. If he hadn't been so scared, Virgil would have been lapping up the attention.

As they walked, Charlie ran through the game plan: "Once we've reversed the wormhole's polarity, there's no way of measuring how quickly it will close. It could stay open for several more minutes. Or it could vanish instantaneously. And even if we do make it back alive, there's no guarantee that we'll return *exactly* to the point in time we exited from."

"Aye, aye, Señor Positivo," Virgil joked. He felt obligated to inject a moment of brevity into what might be their last minutes.

Zeke was bombarded by the two girls from Space Burger—the "Zeke Freaks," as they called themselves. They hugged him as Amy Fox also broke through the barricade and approached Virgil.

"I heard you were trying to save the world," she said.

"That's right," said Virgil cockily. "Your big brother's cool, huh?"

"When you die, can I have your room? Mine's way too small and—"

"Bye, Amy," Virgil said, cutting her off.

Jeanette ran up to Charlie and flung her arms around his neck. "Come back in one piece, okay, Charlie?"

She smiled and planted a huge kiss on his lips.

He froze, his lips staying in a pucker even after she left. Zeke had to pick him up and carry him off toward the vortex.

And then it was Stephanie's turn. She anxiously approached Virgil.

"Listen, Steph," Virgil started, "even if I do make it back okay, there's a chance that . . . things between us will be . . ."

"Verge," she said, stopping him, "it will work out. You and I are meant to be."

Emboldened by her words, Virgil pulled Stephanie into his arms. And then, in front of the huge crowd, he kissed her. The crowd cheered, thundering "Min-ute-men! Min-ute-men!"

Virgil and Stephanie broke their kiss and stared at each other for a moment. Suddenly, something registered.

"Hey!" Virgil said brightly. "They got the name right!"

Stephanie laughed, squeezed his hand, and joined Jeanette back by the barriers. The Minutemen, nearing the giant vortex, turned for one last look at the crowd. It was Go Time.

Holding tight to their portable time machine, they jumped simultaneously into the gaping hole. "YEEEEEEEEE-HAAAAAAA!" they yelled, disappearing.

Chapter Twenty-five

The wormhole was a kaleidoscopic roller coaster of color and light as the boys hurtled through space and time.

Then suddenly, there were three big thuds as the Minutemen fell seemingly out of the trees. They could hear the sounds of children playing nearby. Charlie, on his back, looked up at the tree from which they'd fallen. Judging from the reds and oranges of the leaves, it was autumn. That was a good sign.

Suddenly, with a bright flash, the portable time machine appeared, landing hard on the ground beside them.

Standing and brushing themselves off, the

guys looked around at the children who had heard the noise and quickly surrounded them. Their mouths hung open in large O's. "Space men!" one of them whispered in awe.

"I think we landed in Munchkin Land," Virgil told Zeke, under his breath.

"Actually," said Charlie, "we're across town at the elementary school."

Above them, in the branches of the tree, the swirling vortex was growing, getting larger and larger. They didn't have much time.

"What planet did you come from? Are you from Neptune?" a little boy asked, clinging to Virgil's pant leg. "Do people on Neptune eat macaroni? I love macaroni!"

"Beat it, kid. We're workin' here," Virgil said, brushing him aside.

They had to get busy on the machine. Zeke was already attaching a portable generator. He flipped a switch and the machine lit up.

"Beginning reversal sequence . . ." said Charlie.

He flipped more switches, and a second vortex, swirling in the opposite direction, blasted upward, stabilizing the first one. The kids went bananas.

"Rate of increase is slowing," Charlie said excitedly. "Just hold it steady for a couple more seconds . . ."

His handheld computer beeped loudly. "Stabilization achieved!" he yelled. "The polarity is decreasing. . . . I think we did it!"

The Minutemen high-fived. Virgil spotted a newspaper rack on the other side of the playground fence. He leaned over to read the date. "Yo, guys," he called. "Today is September third, 2004." They had gone further back than ever before.

"The first day of school, freshman year," Charlie said, realization dawning.

"So that's the day of . . ." Zeke started.

". . . the Incident," Charlie and Virgil finished, nodding.

"Of course!" Charlie said, hitting his forehead with the palm of his hand. "This was the day that a module of quantum acceleration first interacted with the space-time continuum!"

Virgil and Zeke looked at him, lost.

"The rocket lawn mower, remember?" Charlie continued. "It's linked the wormhole from our present to this moment in the past."

"What time is it?" Virgil asked suddenly.

Charlie glanced at his fancy watch. "It's 2:33. At this very moment," he said wistfully, "our younger selves are being tied to the mascot and publicly humiliated. . . ."

Charlie looked up to see Virgil not listening, but instead sprinting away, toward the football field. Charlie and Zeke took off after him.

Reaching the top of the hill, Virgil watched as a familiar scene unraveled below—a scene that had played out in his mind a million times before.

Football tryouts. Fourteen-year-old Virgil talks with fourteen-year-old Derek. From the side of the field comes skinny, eleven-year-old Charlie, riding an out-of-control lawn mower. Chaos erupts as he nears the pack of players.

"Don't do it," Virgil whispered to his younger

self. He started to run down the hill, but quickly found himself tackled by Zeke.

Charlie ran up, out of breath. "You're honestly thinking of stopping what's going on down there?!" he gasped.

"Why not?" asked Virgil as Zeke released him. "Isn't that what the Minutemen do? Undo mistakes? Well, I made a mistake down there."

"We don't have time!" Charlie reminded him. They had to jump back through the vortex before it completely closed, or they'd be trapped forever.

"But I still have a chance to be somebody," Virgil said desperately. "To be popular." He started back down the hill.

Charlie looked crestfallen. "Okay, but know this. . . . What happened down there is . . . we became friends. That day that we were tied up together on that stupid ram statue—THIS DAY, this day that you hate so much because you got a little embarrassed—is my *favorite* day."

Virgil stopped and turned to look at Charlie.

Down on the field, a young Derek was tossing a Hail Mary that struck young Charlie on the head, knocking him off the lawn mower. Young Virgil jogged toward him.

"Even though I'd still be a nerd," Charlie went on, "it didn't really matter anymore, because now I had a real friend. And that would always make everything okay. . . . But so much for 'always,'" he said bitterly, kicking at the grass. He turned and started the long walk back to the elementary school and the vortex.

"Listen, Verge," said Zeke, before turning to follow Charlie, "you do what you gotta do here. And if things aren't the same on the other side? Well, it's been a good ride."

Virgil stood for a moment, torn. He imagined what his life might look like had the Incident never happened . . . the parties, the girls, the cool friends. Then he looked back at the figures of Zeke and Charlie receding into the distance.

Young Derek's voice echoed up from the field. "You guys shouldn't do that . . ." Derek was saying.

Virgil turned to see his old friend in the middle of a huddle of football players. Was Derek sticking up for him?

". . . What would be better is smearing lipstick on those idiots."

Nope.

Virgil shook his head and was thankful for his friends—his *true* friends—Charlie and Zeke.

Chapter Twenty-six

*B*EEP! *BEEP! BEEP!* The sound startled
Charlie as he walked, downtrodden, back across
town with Zeke. It was his handheld computer.
Charlie pulled it from his pocket, and his face
turned a ghostly white.

"The closure rate of the vortex just went into
overdrive!" he exclaimed. "RUN!"

Charlie and Zeke began racing toward the
elementary school.

"What about Virgil?!" Zeke yelled as they
ran.

"There's no way we could make it to him and
back in time!"

They could just barely see the playground in

the distance. It was empty now, the children all gone. What they couldn't see yet was that high in the trees, the vortex was fluctuating violently. With a loud slurping noise, it sucked up the time machine. It was getting smaller and smaller with each burst of light.

Charlie tripped and slammed onto the pavement, ripping the silver suit at his knees and scraping his hands. Zeke helped him up.

"We're never going to make it. We're almost a mile away. . . . We're stuck in the past forever!" Charlie cried in horror.

As he said this, the buzz of an engine ripped through the quiet neighborhood. Charlie and Zeke looked up to see Virgil, zooming toward them on the old rocket lawn mower.

"Man, you guys do *not* want to go back there," Virgil said with a grin when he caught up. "These two kids are being roughed up by a bunch of football players. It's real ugly."

"You don't say?" Charlie smiled.

"It's true that a person's life can change in a single moment," said Virgil. "But maybe—who knows—in the end, we wind up where we're supposed to be."

Virgil stuck out his hand, and for the first time ever, Charlie got the handshake right. "Scorch!" he and Virgil yelled.

"Uh, guys," said Zeke, glancing nervously toward the vortex in the distance, "your handshake is cute and all, but we gotta move."

Charlie and Zeke climbed aboard and blasted off, blowing past startled citizens on the sidewalk. Cars screeched as the lawn mower ripped through a busy intersection, closing in on the cluster of trees where the vortex had shrunk to only a couple feet in diameter.

"We've got to hit the vortex moving," Virgil yelled to Charlie behind him, "and that means airborne. We'll come up over that big hill to catch some air."

"Virgil," Charlie screamed into the wind, "we just overshot the hill!"

Virgil's face dropped.

"No problem," Zeke shouted. "We're taking a corner."

In one smooth motion, Zeke whipped out his grappling hook, swung it above his head, and lassoed it around a lamppost. It hooked, and the lawn mower made a sharp U-turn, hitting the hill just right and catapulting into the air.

"See you guys in the future!" Virgil hollered.

Each Minuteman passed through the closing hole before it sealed shut and disappeared. The lawn mower was not so lucky. It plummeted through the branches and crashed to the ground, wheels spinning.

Chapter Twenty-seven

Sweaty, unhappy students trudged along Summerton High School's track as Coach Nibley yelled and checked his stopwatch.

Out of the blue, a blast of light charged the sky and, from a momentary swirling vortex, three snowsuit-clad figures were spit out and hurled to the ground. A moment later, what looked like a souped-up slide projector followed, shattering on the ground. Then the vortex disappeared—forever.

Virgil, Charlie, and Zeke sat up, dazed.

"What day is it?" asked Virgil.

"I have no idea," answered Zeke, rubbing his bruised behind.

"Okay, get up," Coach Nibley demanded, spotting the boys sitting on the ground. "Nobody loafs in my gym class."

"You don't understand . . ." Charlie started.

"GO! GO! GO!" Nibley yelled.

The boys jumped to their feet and started running around the track as Nibley admired their white jogging suits.

Charlie ran up to Zeke and Virgil after gym. "Guys, I just found out what day it is," he said. "It's the first day that we time-traveled. The day we tried to win the lottery."

"Charlie, that can't be right. Otherwise, we'd run into versions of ourselves," said Virgil.

"No, here's what I'm thinking," Charlie explained excitedly. "The versions of us you'd think are walking around right now—aren't. That's because there's only *this* version of us. You see, this day hasn't happened yet."

"Uh . . . yeah, it has," insisted Virgil.

"No, Virgil. Our current forms have a memory of this day, but at this point, that's nothing more than a dream. Back in the past, we entered a wormhole at its maximum limit before closure. Therefore, on this side of the space-time continuum . . ."

". . . We're free and clear," finished Zeke.

They rounded a corner to find Vice Principal Tolkan breaking up a group of loitering students. He gave an uninterested, "whatever" glance at the three boys in white snowsuits and returned to his lecture.

"Huh," Virgil said. Maybe they *were* free and clear.

"I said, 'My boyfriend is a lying cheese brain. . . .'"

Stephanie sat at a library table as the familiar scene played out. Derek was lamely trying to convince her his only interest in Jocelyn was for her French skills.

"Nice outfits, bozos," Derek scoffed as he passed the Minutemen on his way out.

"Hey, Derek," Virgil said slyly, "say hi to Jocelyn for me."

Derek gave him a panicked look. "What's that supposed to mean? You know something?"

Virgil said nothing and headed for Stephanie. Charlie and Zeke hung back. Zeke spotted the "Zeke Freaks" sitting at another table. He gave them a tiny nod. "Ladies," he said smoothly.

Jeanette, her arms full of books, approached. "Hey Sugar Flakes," she winked at Charlie. "Now you *really* look like a cereal-box action doll," she said, gesturing appreciatively at the silver suit.

"Thanks, pumpkin," Charlie said nonchalantly, planting a kiss on her.

Jeanette freaked. "What are you doing?"

"Bro," Zeke said in a low voice, "remember, you haven't kissed her before."

Charlie freaked, too. "Jeanette." He began to stammer. "I didn't mean . . . I was just . . ."

Jeanette hurried off with a tiny smile on her face. Not bad, she thought.

Virgil took a seat across from Stephanie. "Uh, Steph," he asked uncertainly, "you didn't see me in here before, did you?"

"No . . . and what's with the shiny suit?" She looked at him strangely.

Virgil thought fast. "Actually, I was just

rehearsing a little school play about time travel, and it got me thinking . . . if I could really go back in time, what would I change?"

"That snowsuit?" Stephanie laughed.

"I would tell Stephanie how I really feel about her, that I think she's great."

Stephanie blushed, taken aback. "Really?"

"Yep."

"And if I could go back in time," she said, a smile playing on her lips, "I think I'd tell Virgil the same."

They locked eyes across the table.

"So," Virgil asked, "are you free after school?"

"I don't know, Verge . . ." Stephanie teased, "what's going to happen if I say yes?"

"That's the great thing about the future," Virgil answered, glancing back to Charlie and Zeke, "you just never know. Right, guys?"

They grinned. "Totally."